Real Ghost Stories of Borneo 2

True and Real First Accounts

of Ghost Encounters

By

Dr. Aammton Alias

Copyright ©2018 Aammton Alias, M Content Creations
All Rights Reserved

Cover design by Aammton Alias

ISBN: 978-0-359-31223-8

Please visit my website at http://www.b1percent.com

Permission to reproduce or transmit in any form or by any means, electronic or mechanical, including photocopying and recording, or by an information storage and retrieval system, must be obtained by writing to the author via email:

author@b1percent.com

For enquiries on obtaining printed books, please email: now@b1percent.com

Contents Page

Acknowledgments *6*
Hello Again! *7*
The Refuge of Love *10*
A Father's Daughter *17*
Respect *24*
The Joggers & The Hills *37*
The Attack *43*
The Welcome *51*
Ride to Kuching *56*
1964 .... *62*
Flash *71*
The Seru *76*
The Longhouse *81*
Best Friends Forever *85*
Tear in the Fabric *89*
Mount Singai *93*
Intruder & The Conspiracy *99*
Left Behind *109*
Fisherman's Tale *115*

The Twins 124

The Drive 128

The Crossing 136

The Room 141

The Keeper 149

Skylight 156

The Shadow 161

The Car 165

The Kem 171

The Calling 179

The Fitting 183

The On-call Room 187

Teluki 192

About The Author 198

My Other Books 199

*Dedicated to the unnamed truth-seekers
who toil through the long dark night*

Acknowledgments

I could not have written this book without the two most important women in my life: my wife and my 18-year-old daughter. They have both supported me heartily in my writing. They would check my stories and would be the first to give valuable feedback. They encouraged me when I was down and made me copious amounts of coffee on demand!

I am most grateful and continue to be indebted to the first or 'alpha' readers which includes my ten-year-old son, who helped provide honest and crucial feedback in order to make this book happen.

I thank the story contributors for this second book, in particular 'Bob', Adrina Hj Mohd Agus Din, Iswardy Morni, Wilhelm Bayona, as well as Rabiatul Mohamad and her students. I also thank the many contributors who chose to remain anonymous.

Bob continues to show me the path and provides me support in realising my full writing potential.

Finally, I thank the support of my compatriots in the Reading & Literacy Association (RELA). Together we will instill the reading and writing culture amongst our people.

Hello Again!

It gives me great pleasure to make this book 'Real Ghost Stories of Borneo 2' available to you. The first Real Ghost Stories of Borneo turned out to be quite popular and I was compelled to write the second book as there were a few stories that I could not include in the first book. In addition to that, I had several people who were keen to share their ghostly encounters. Most were personally interviewed by myself whilst others sent in their submissions through social media and mobile messaging (WhatsApp & Telegram). There were times when I thought I could not make this book become a reality. I kept reminding my team and I, that 'we had to complete the mission.' So here we are again. If there was a theme for this particular book then it would be 'travel and places'!

If you haven't read the first book, please do get a copy - beg, borrow or steal - okay maybe not the last option. The stories in both books are focused on supernatural encounters in the northern part of Borneo i.e. Sabah, Brunei and Sarawak. Unfortunately, I do not have any friends or associates from Kalimantan, but that is something I am looking forward to. You will notice that the ghost sightings and experiences may differ from those in West Malaysia and elsewhere in Southeast Asia. I have some insights on why. (I wonder if you have the same speculations too.)

I must warn you that several of the stories do not have happy endings whilst others seem to have an open ending with no firm explanation. That is simply the way it was experienced and told. Perhaps the person(s) involved in the encounter may discover the true reasons and meaning in the future.

This book has had a good response with the pre-order campaign. Pre-orders made this book possible and it helped bring costs down. I humbly thank you for believing in my efforts. I hope this book fulfills or beats your expectations.

This book is not meant to encourage ghost hunting. Remember, it is important to 'be aware' and not bother them. Our worlds are meant to be separated, though, it is clear that 'infractions' occur from time to time.

Once again, I thank all the contributors for their stories, and I hope you will continue to support my efforts to record more of our stories and encounters.

If you wish to share your ghost encounters and stories for the next book, please feel free to contact me @aammton (Instagram) and yes all my contact details are at the back of the book. Please check 'About The Author' chapter.

This book was published with the help of friends and family. With pride, we pour our hearts to produce the best quality for this book. If you do find any mistake(s), please accept my sincerest apologies and please do let me know.

I thank you for buying this book and supporting my work and the works of others. Producing the first book was a joy and this second book has been an even greater joy.

I hope you enjoy reading this book and all the little frights it brings you!

The Refuge of Love

My uncle, Nas, worked all his life in the oil and gas industry. He was one of those uncles I had considered as 'macho'. He had a long, thick mustache that somehow seemed to groom itself and he always projected himself as an immovable and undaunted character. I remember when I was 12, I had somehow asked him if he was afraid of anything. I didn't expect him to say yes...

One evening in the 1980s, Nas had finished his grueling work schedule for the week and decided to go back to his parents' home. He was keen to get home as he was quite eager to meet up with his girlfriend. However, he got distracted by his friends and ended up playing rounds of darts with them. It was already late night by the time they had finished. Nas was not a superstitious man. He wore his black leather jacket and jumped on his beautiful silver red sports motorbike, a Suzuki Katana. He loved the way the engine hummed, purred and then roared to life as it brought him to wherever he desired.

It was the start of a beautiful night ride. The stars twinkled in the black background whilst the full moon glowed brightly, luminescing on to the asphalt road. There were no streetlights back then, so Nas was very grateful for the lights. He imagined the sweet smile of his girlfriend as he sped through the white silica sand area of Tutong, famously known as 'Pasir Puteh'. His eyes should have stayed on the road in front of him, but they would occasionally wander at the white sandy area. Nas appreciated how the moonlight gave a surreal effect on the landscape, which was dotted with shrubs, bushes and a few short trees.

Suddenly, the moon luminescence disappeared and darkness overwhelmed the surrounding land. The motorcycle's yellow-orange light flickered for a moment. Nas revved the engine faster and the bike's light shone brighter. Nas wasn't alarmed. He thought the darkness was probably a large cloud overshadowing the area. He scoffed off any paranoid thoughts.

It was at this exact moment Nas felt a force hit him. He lost control and both the bike and himself slid on the road and then crashed.

Nas did not know how long he was unconscious for. He thought he was out for only a few seconds. Lying flat on his back on the white silica sand, he did his best to get back on his feet. His body was sore all over, and he could feel a sharp knife-like pain in his left knee. He patted his body to check if he had broken any bones. Luckily, he seemed intact. Nas's helmet had also protected his head from any serious injuries. Nas slowly took off his helmet and looked around. He could see his motorcycle's dimming headlight, showing the bike was nearby and entangled hopelessly in a shrub. Limping his way towards it, he did his best to shift his weight on to his right knee. It seemed like ages before he finally reached his bike.

Nas struggled as he propped up his silver red motorbike whilst pulling the shrub strands and branches away from its body and engine. The bike seemed much heavier than before. He inspected it in the dim light and thought the motorcycle had not suffered any serious damage.

He slowly pushed his motorcycle back onto the road. He tried to restart the engine but it was to no avail. He tried to start the engine with the headlights switched off and then on, but nothing worked. Each futile attempt caused the headlight to dim even further until there was completely no life in the whole machine.

Rage filled Nas as he pushed his bike back off the road. He looked at his watch, it was 2am. The chance of hitching a ride from a passerby would be zero, simply because no one would drive across this area at this twilight time, and anyone who would do so would probably be too scared to pick up a complete stranger at this time and place. He cursed himself for not leaving earlier. After he had calmed himself down, he changed his perspective and convinced himself to be grateful for surviving a motorcycle crash. Nas formulated a plan. There were no mobile phones, no text messages and no WhatsApp. There were no pay-phones nearby. He would have to sleep it rough right there on the white sand, away from the shrubs and the short trees. Once it was dawn, he would stop any passing cars and hitch a ride home.

Nas took off his leather jacket and bundled it to form a makeshift pillow. He laid on the sand and closed his eyes. It was not long after that he was awoken by a loud crackling sound in the air. It was the distinct sound of fire. Nas jumped on to his feet expecting to find himself surrounded by fire. Instead he found nothing but a small fire burning in the shrub where he had crashed his motorcycle. Nas thought it was strange as it sounded very loud for a small fire. He approached the burning shrub and as he got close, Nas became puzzled. The flames were bright dark red and each flame danced on its own. He put his hand towards it and felt no warmth from it.

Nas thought what a strange fire, if it was a fire. It looked very much alive, as though its individual flames were waving to him. He wondered if he was dreaming. He looked back to the spot where he was sleeping. Then he looked back at the cold fire, and when he did that, something had caught the corner of his eye.

He could see a large shadow moving across the darkness. He chose to ignore it and was about to head back to his sleeping spot, when the moonlight lit up the surrounding area. At that moment, Nas held his breath and his heart raced wildly in his chest. In the white-gray sandy landscape, he saw hundreds of tall giant humanoid creatures wandering around the area. They were at least twice his height and he noticed they had no facial features.

He froze still, hoping that they would not notice him. He watched them without moving his head, his eyes frantically scanning. To his horror, one of the dark tall creatures took interest in him. It paused for a moment. Nas wondered if it was curious about him, and yet everything about his onlooker shook his core and warned him of great danger. It let out an ear-piercing scream and the other creatures began to head towards him.

Nas ran away from his first onlooker, pushing through his pain threshold and doing his best not to stumble onto the soft crumbling sandy ground. His steps felt heavier every time he tried to run faster. The giant faceless demons were everywhere, there were probably hundreds of them that he could see. He did not know where to run to, there was no shelter to run to. Sprinting scatteringly in ever-changing directions, he was about to give up hope when he heard a shrill familiar female voice in his head.

"Run here, quick!"

Without thinking much, he knew immediately the voice came from the 'burning shrub.' He ran as fast as his injured legs could take him and slid into the bright red flames. The fire did not burn him, but instead bathe him with a warm radiance. The giant tall creatures surrounded the burning shrub but did not dare approach it too closely.

Although the dark creatures robed in darkness had no facial features and no apparent eyes, Nas could feel their evil intent burning through his heart. Nas did not budge from the shrub. Eventually, the demons lost interest in him and carried on with their seemingly aimless wandering. Nas did not move from that shrub, he was not taking any chances. He clung onto his life until he fell asleep.

When Nas woke up, it was already a bright morning. He hailed a passing car, which brought him to his friend's place. His friend, who owned a pickup truck, and himself came back to the same place and hauled his motorbike. Upon inspection, he noticed the engine had been badly damaged. There was no way it could have restarted without some serious repairs at the workshop. His friend picked up his helmet, which was almost split in two. Laughing hard and reminding Nas how lucky he was, he couldn't figure out what Nas could have hit to cause such damage.

When Nas finally came back home, his girlfriend Nana came around immediately. She was quite anxious and was very worried for Nas. She mentioned that the night before, she had a nightmare about Nas being surrounded by tall faceless demons. In her dream, she was fending off the demons from devouring his soul. Nas didn't immediately tell her what he had experienced, especially since he realised the female voice he heard coming from the shrub sounded very much like his girlfriend's.

Nas married her soon after that accident. Nas never rode a motorbike again.

Nas would never travel alone across the white sands of Tutong in the middle of the night.

A Father's Daughter

By Amal (not her real name)

The local female author of this story had chosen to remain anonymous for understandable reasons.

This story is about my late father who passed away in 2016. The pain of losing him still aches to this day. I was always close to my father.

You see, my father was a white 'magic' healer. He spent his life helping people and friends who had problems dealing with the supernatural. Growing up in the family, I myself was a witness to the 'work' my father had done.

Over the years, my father accumulated a few 'souvenirs'. He would tell me that some of these items would have their own 'inhabitants'. My mother and I would usually get nervous every time we walked past his 'storage' area. There was an uncomfortable presence that we could feel and yet could not explain.

One day, my father became very unwell. He became weaker and weaker with each passing day. Doctors could not figure out why he was unwell. They could not give us a diagnosis, let alone a prognosis. Eventually, a family friend recommended a spiritual healer to us. This was strange, as my father himself was a magic healer, and now in his time of need, we would need the help of another healer.

We have never met this healer before. His name was Awang and strangely enough, he had prosthetic legs. We told him what had happened and that my father was in the Intensive Care Unit (ICU) of the main hospital. Awang wanted to see my father immediately, but insisted that we stop over at our house first. The moment we arrived home and parked at the driveway, Awang acted strangely. He said he could sense something.

Now, I would like to remind you that this man had prosthetic legs and was initially walking (barely) with a cane. Awang got out and ran towards the back of our house. That's right, he ran and he was fast. My mother and I stood there in shock.

When he came back Awang explained, "I was trying to catch 'It' but it ran away."

After a breather, he went cautiously around the house. It was like he was inspecting something. We watched him whilst he began asking us several questions. One of the questions he asked was whether we have been hearing children laughing and any unexplained howling. The hairs at the back of our necks stood up, as this was something that although we had both experienced, we would never talk about.

We spent about three hours around the house before he began to inspect my father's favourite area, his orchids. There, this man sensed danger and he reached into one of my father's potted plants. With his bare hands, he grabbed a large black cobra and then killed it. It was definitely not a pretty sight, and that was when he began to explain that the snake was no ordinary snake.

Awang explained to us this creature was 'sent' to kill my father!

At this point, my mother felt it was too much for her to handle. The presence of the 'cobra' had shaken her badly. She insisted on leaving the house and visiting my father. The house 'inspection' was not yet complete, so I had to remain with Awang.

Awang was able to find something that none of us knew about. He found a set of bison horns on a plaque. It was tucked away in one of the storage rooms. It was strange as the horns were hung neatly behind a shelf, in a room that no one would visit.

When we brought it out of the storeroom, Awang told me to set it out on a stool and he began to look at it closely. I could see a pair of red eyes emerge from the bison's skull. Awang explained that there was something evil inside. The 'inhabitant' of this bison horns was a 'Jinn' that my father had unknowingly nurtured for over 30 years. The Jinn would get stronger by sucking up the life-force of my already weakened father.

Awang began to recite verses from the Holy Quran and then he told me that we would need to throw away the horns into the nearest river. We drove to one that was about 6-7 miles away from our house. I did not have the courage to carry out the task, so Awang - the healer with the prosthetic legs - was the one who had to do the deed. I watched as the bison horns fell down into the river - it was like time had slowed down. As soon as the bison horns sunk and disappeared from vision, we both heard a distant faint scream.

Then my mother called me on my phone. She was frantic, as I heard in the background, my father was screaming that his legs were on fire. The doctors had to heavily sedate him.

At that point, we knew we were still not done yet. Awang asked where else my father had kept his 'collections'. He told me there was one more item that had 'isi' or 'spiritual content' that was as strong as the bison horns. We had to get rid of that immediately. He searched and found certain items but it was the one item that he found that had given us a real scare - a genuine samurai sword or 'katana' owned by a World War 2 Japanese soldier during the Japanese occupation of Brunei. The katana was allegedly used to kill many people including the life of the owner, who would rather take his own life than die in the hands of 'Japanese traitors'. Dumbfounded, we both began to wonder how the heck was my father able to accumulate all these exotic items.

Awang told me that I would have to cut the tip of the samurai sword in order to let the vengeful spirit inside to be released. Then I would have to bury the sword deep into the ground.

Once the healer was done with our house, he insisted on seeing my father immediately in the hospital. My father who was supposed to be heavily sedated, sat up immediately when Awang had arrived. The two of them began to converse in a language that none of us could make out. Towards the end of the conversation, Awang placed his right hand on my father's forehead and recited a few Holy Verses.

He then told my father to rest. My father seemed quite calm and serene. Awang excused himself and then asked me to send him back home.

On our way back to Awang's house, he told me that I may have a strange enigmatic dream that night. He told me that if I dreamt of a burning castle at the back of our house, then I would inherit some of my father's 'skills'.

True enough and unfortunately, that night I dreamt of a burning castle right in my backyard. It was surreal. I remember I could feel the intense heat in my dream. I woke up in a cold sweat and that was when I started to feel 'weird'. I rang Awang immediately and he told me not to worry as these 'things' would not harm me. The castle that burned down was the 'home' to many of these spirits and creatures that have been harassing my father in his dreams.

My father lived on for a few more months before he finally passed away. The only comfort I had was that he died peacefully in his sleep in the ICU ward. We were all devastated. He was my role model, my best friend and my hero, and losing him was really hard for me.

The night he died, I dreamt I saw my father in a white robe with a white hat. He did not utter a single word. He merely smiled and in that sweet silence, I knew what he was trying to say. He was telling me that I would always be his daughter and he was sorry for what he had put us through.

I cried so much in my dream and woke up in tears. I consoled myself by acknowledging that his suffering was over and he seemed a lot happier.

It didn't end there for me though. It turned out one of my father's 'skills' which I have acquired or inherited was the gift of 'second' sight where I sensed and saw 'things' that normal humans can't.

I began to see glimpses of the spirits, in their many forms, things beyond our comprehension. Every now and then I would have dreams where my father would tell me that I will be safe and alright.

For some unknown compelling reason, I gathered enough courage to write this on a 'Friday' night where most of these 'beings' tend to wander a lot, but writing this story has made me feel much better and I hope I'll be able to move on from it.

A photo of the bison's horns before it was disposed off

Respect

Although he had been living in Brunei most of his life, Jon did not know much about his country. He had been busy with pursuing his studies all his life and never went out much. After graduating from the UK, he came back to Brunei and started work as a civil engineer. Jon was tall for a local man and he had Eurasian facial features, which made him stand out even more amongst his kinsmen. He had always wanted to fit in but he never did.

After living in the UK for some time, he felt the differences between his people and himself were widening. Everyone kept on asking if he was a Bruneian or not. It was getting annoying and Jon felt that life was becoming unbearable.

Somehow, he had met a group of expats who were keen snorkelers and decided to join them on their snorkeling excursions.

At first, the group went snorkeling at the three small islands off Labuan island. The first was Kuraman island. The name Kuraman actually meant corpse, as the long island looked like a lying corpse. However, there was not much to see as the coral had been obliterated through years of fish-bombing and cyanide use. Cyanide was used to stun coral fish, which were later sold to aquariums.

The other island was Rusukan Besar. It was a small island that you could swim around in over less than an hour. Sometimes, the water was crystal clear and at some places, the coral was vibrant. Jon and the group could see black-tipped reef sharks, which was a beauty to see. There were shoals of colorful fishes, but the current would sometimes be too strong. The boat ride back home was occasionally choppy. The third island Rusukan Kecil, which itself was much smaller than Rusukan Besar, had very few coral spots left. It was more of a place to have a short private picnic. By right, these islands belong to Malaysia and one would always have to bring his/her passport - just in case.

Eventually, the group found out about a better snorkeling site, which was Pelong Rocks or Pelong Island.

Pelong Rocks was no ordinary island. It was a string of large rock formations that rose out of the sea. At the centre, the water was shallow enough that you could stand in the waist-deep water, whilst the water around it was deep and yet clear. Hard corals lined the entire area and numerous colourful coral fishes could be found here. It was very near to Meragang Beach, which meant that it was a shorter boat ride in a much calmer sea. There was a small automated lighthouse tower on the main rock (Pelong South), with a few trees and vines growing wildly there.

Jon was excited to snorkel at Pelong Rocks. His friends and himself made plans to have a post-snorkeling barbecue at Pelumpong island, as Pelong rocks had no beach or sandy area.

It was the start of a beautiful day. The sky was deep blue and had a few low-hanging clouds. Jon and his friends were on the boat, heading straight to Pelong Rocks, enjoying the cruise as the seawater; from time to time, would spray onto their faces. Jon loved being with his expat friends as they were very open-minded and adventurous. Jon compared them to his countrymen who were always holding themselves back, constrained by superstitions and always awaiting the approval of others before taking any action.

There was another reason why he loved being with this group of expat friends. Jon was very attracted to Ruth; a petite American woman with auburn hair who loved to snorkel and dive. A plutonic friendship for two people who did not want to think about the future. Jon had secretly wished for more, but never had the courage to step up in the relationship. He didn't want to risk losing their friendship. And that was how things were. Everyone was savoring the moment, with the sea breeze in their hair. No one thought this trip would bring any of them tragedy.

The boat stopped in front of the mysterious rock formation. Some imagined they were actually at the Galapagos Islands, as it looked like that - at least for those who had never been there and merely seen the photos of the Galapagos Islands. Nevertheless, this was their 'Galapagos Islands'. The seven of them looked down and saw the water was turquoise blue and crystal clear. It was about 4 meters deep, yet they could see everything from the sandy floor, the rock formations, the coral and the fishes that zoomed pass by, below the boat. All of them were confident swimmers, so water depth was never an issue.

It seemed like forever that everyone stood there, mesmerised by the beauty of the rock island and the clear water. The sound of one of Jon's friends jumping into the water broke that spell. Laughter ensued, and one by one, everyone wore their snorkeling gear and jumped into the water.

"After you, Ruth. Ladies first." Jon thought he was being chivalrous whilst at the same time, he wanted to be the one to watch Ruth jump out. Ruth was wearing a blue swimsuit and she looked stunning, as the sun rays sparkled on the water behind her.

"Beauty before age, I suppose." She smiled teasingly at him as she jumped feet first into the water. Jon had an adrenaline rush that brought him to a new high. He was keen to show Ruth his physical prowess. He put on his diving fins, mask and snorkel. Jon was about to jump into the water head first, when a firm hand held him back.

He turned around; it was the boat skipper.

"Bro, I realised you don't remember me. It's me Rizhar."

Rizhar was a childhood friend. Rizhar and Jon used to be neighbours and schoolmates. There was a time when they used to be close but everyone seemed to drift apart as they grew older and pursued their dreams.

"Hey Rizhar, it's been a long time." Jon didn't continue the conversation. He had someone to catch up to and frolic in the sun - or at least that was the idea. His body language revealed his annoyance. Rizhar understood the 'bro code'.

"Don't worry, Jon. We'll catch up next time, but I must warn you, this is not an ordinary place. Be wary - remember the 'pantangs' - and do recite a prayer before you start your fun."

Jon scoffed in reflex as he pushed himself off the boat and entered the cool seawater. Jon thought, why should he care about the pantangs or taboos. He was the prime manifestation of the modern Brunei man.

Jon orientated himself and then bobbed his head out of the water. He figured he had to seem like he was swimming unintentionally towards Ruth. Jon set his direction towards her and started snorkeling.

He might as well enjoy the sight, he thought. He observed several large barrel coral and the purple, green and red hard coral growing on the various large rocks. Occasionally, he would stop and look above the water to see how near he was to Ruth. The current had picked up and was pushing him away from Ruth. The sun was getting brighter and as it filtered through the clear water, patterns played themselves out on the sand, on the rocks and all over the coral.

Jon noted that one pattern was not moving like the others. It remained constant. He swam closer towards it, as it happened to be in the direction he was swimming towards. He immediately recognised the pattern. He gasped and then shook his head in the water.

"No, it couldn't be!" Jon thought he saw a face in one of the underwater rock formations. There was no doubting it, it seemed like a sleeping face with closed eyes. It had a short nose and a closed mouth. Jon reasoned it was a formation in the rock, likely from a strange erosive pattern. The moment he had concluded this logic, he saw the face moved. It opened its eyes and he could see a pair of black vacant eyes staring at him, and the lips moved as though trying to say something to him.

A great panic surged into Jon. He swam away, kicking with his fins as hard and as fast as he could. Jon's mind was racing with a hundred questions. What was that thing that he just saw? What did it want from him? He didn't swim far from that same spot as the current surged against him. He looked down and he could see several small fishes near the seabed below him, swimming hard and yet remaining in the same spot! There was also a strong underwater current. Jon swam for his life, pushing himself hard to a point he was near the main group where Ruth was.

Ruth could sense there was something wrong with Jon.

She swam close to him, "Are you alright?"

"I thought I saw something strange in the water," Jon replied. He was careful about what to say. Suddenly, Jon was very superstitious.

"What did you see?" Ruth was curious.

"Oh never mind, it's not important." Jon realised this was not the best place to talk about these things.

His mind was pre-occupied with what he had seen, and he kept his distance from Ruth, whilst remaining close by. He pretended to be engaged with snorkeling. Jon wanted to get out of the place quickly, and yet pride kept him there.

As the group swam close to a rock wall, they could see an abundance of sea life: fishes and soft and hard coral formations. There, to his horror, Jon saw the same face on a bare patch of the rock wall. Black eyes with the same vacant stare. Jon swam away from the group and headed towards the boat. He figured it must be some sort of optical illusion. He convinced himself that what he saw was not real. He took off his mask, and continued swimming towards the boat whilst keeping his head above the water. The gentle waves lapped on to his face and the seawater constantly stung his sunburnt face. He reasoned, at least he didn't have to see it. If he didn't look underwater then he could not see that damned face.

As he got halfway towards the boat, he heard a deep voice behind him. Jon turned around and saw a head floating on the water. It was the same face with the black eyes staring at him, it made a low grumbling sound. Its hair was disheveled and wet.

Jon yelled out as he pushed off with all his four limbs against it. The floating head did not pursue him as he kept himself a good distance away from it. Jon was preoccupied with the floating head that he did not notice a large rogue wave heading towards him. The wave caught Jon by surprise; it pushed Jon under the water as he struggled to swim up. He was a good swimmer and yet Jon felt his efforts were futile.

Jon eventually got to the surface, catching his breath and letting the current take him close to the island. He was exhausted and could barely float. The waves brought Jon into a small inlet on the rock island. The water churned foamy white, which Jon knew was a dangerous thing. It meant that the water was very turbulent. Jon was now trapped inside the inlet. He could barely stay afloat as his body was spun in a whirlpool of turbulent milky white water. He kicked off as much as he could but he had nothing left. He could see a dark void open up behind him. Jon thought this was the end for him. This was where he would die. That was Jon's last thoughts as a claw sunk into his chest and pulled at his right arm. Jon felt a strong sensation going round his neck and thought no more. He watched the yellow-orange light dance in front of him and onto his face. It sure was warm, he thought.

It was at that moment, Jon realised he had been rescued. He felt with his own hand and recognised another person's arm around his neck. He glanced on his side, it was Rizhar. Rizhar had rescued him from impending death. Rizhar brought Jon onto the boat. Jon was relieved to be back on the boat, slumping unashamedly on the floor.

"You were nearly sucked into that underwater hole. That would have been hard, if not impossible, to get out from," Rizhar laughed out, which contradicted the solemness of his words.

"Thanks Rizhar. I don't know how. I saw a face..." Rizhar stopped Jon mid-sentence. He knew it was best not to talk about it. Jon retched and then vomitted a few times. He must have swallowed quite a bit of salt water. Jon stayed on the boat and kept to himself. By noon, the sun was scorching hot. Everyone got back onto the boat. Ruth was wondering what had happened, but Jon did not tell her anything.

Even during the post-snorkeling barbecue, Jon stayed away from everyone else. Most of the time, he remained on the boat. He wanted to go home quickly. He didn't feel right. Although the island was far away now, he felt very unsettled. Jon fell asleep on the boat and did not wake up until the barbecue was over which was around 4pm. When Jon woke up, he felt more exhausted than before he slept.

The boat eventually brought them back to Serasa Beach. Jon's legs trembled as he stepped on the ground of the mainland. He was very much relieved that he made it back. He shook Rizhar's hand and thanked him. They exchanged phone numbers and promised to catch up. Before getting into his car, Ruth came up to Jon, and asked what had happened. Jon told Ruth everything about the face in the rock, the floating head above the water and his near-death experience in a whirlpool, and that all this happened whilst everyone was enjoying themselves. He could see from her facial expression that she had a hard time believing him. Jon drove off without saying goodbye. He needed to go home, take a shower and sleep and then sort out his thoughts. That was the plan.

Jon got home to his apartment in the city centre. He was going to have a long hot shower. He washed his hair with ample amounts of shampoo. He had to get rid of the salt in his hair. However, this made the shampoo foam cover his eyes. As he washed the shampoo off his hair, he noticed that some segments of his hair had clumped together. The more he tried to straighten it, the more entangled it became. Jon got frustrated; he washed the foam off his face, rubbing his face vigorously and then scrubbing his hair vigorously too. It was maddening for him. A part of him wanted to cut off the entangled hair off. He pulled it hard and realized it did not hurt him. He wondered what it was. He looked at the black clumped hair which seemed quite long and then realised it was hanging from above him!

Jon looked up and collapsed onto the bathroom floor. It was the same head, the same face. This time, it was hanging from the ceiling of his shower room. It had long hair that extended half way down to the floor.

Jon scrambled on the slippery floor as he ran out naked out of the shower. He grabbed a towel and the nearest shorts he could find. He quickly put them on while preparing to hit whatever danger would come to him. He took his phone and car keys and then ran downstairs to his car.

Half-naked, he called up his parents but no one was answering. He thought about calling Ruth but the whole thing was unbelievable. She would think he was crazy. He seemed crazy. Jon remembered Rizhar and called him.

Explaining everything frantically to Rizhar, Rizhar gave his address and suggested he come around.

Unlike Jon's apartment, Rizhar's place was a messy bachelor's pad, which he shared with his co-workers. After calming down and being lent a t-shirt, Jon explained everything and Rizhar listened intently.

"What was it?" Jon asked. Rizhar shrugged. He did not know what it was. Rizhar talked about what he had learned from the island. Rizhar learnt his new motto in life: respect everything, respect the Unseen and the Unexplained.

Over the next few days, Rizhar shared the strange unexplained sightings he had at Pelong Rocks and elsewhere. Jon opened his mind to understanding the Unseen. When he went back to his apartment, there were occasions where he would see the head again, but this time he would chose to ignore it. Or at least pretended to not notice the floating head.

Soon enough, the sightings disappeared completely. Within a few weeks, Jon gathered the courage to experience the Pelong Rocks snorkeling again. This time he went with a group of local yuppies. Ruth and Jon are still close friends to this day. Ruth herself began to believe and understand Jon's experience, as she herself had sightings elsewhere that she could not explain.

The Joggers & The Hills

Nina and Nizam, both in their late 20s, were like the perfect pair. They were both good-looking and physically fit. You could say they were both fitness freaks. They would regularly exercise together in gyms and run together at the Stadium area, with matching designer sports outfits. They considered themselves as the modern Brunei yuppies. (Young Urban Professionals).

There was no doubt that Nina, herself, was very beautiful and she knew that. She also knew that her beauty and her health could disappear any time, which was a source of her insecurity and anxiety. She was constantly worried that her husband would lose interest in her and leave her for another woman. She pushed herself to keep up with her husband's pace.

One day, her husband got very interested in the Bukit Shahbandar Challenge, which was a 9 hill race across the Bukit Shahbandar Forest Recreational Park. One would need physical and mental endurance to compete in this difficult race. Nizam convinced a reluctant Nina to join the Bukit Shahbandar Challenge together as a couple and to train there during the weekends and whenever they both had their afternoons free.

Sometimes Nina wished her husband would be a real sloth at home, especially during the weekends. However, being at home was about watching fitness videos, preparing all kinds of nutrient shakes and talking about improving physical fitness. There was never talk about having children. It was always too early to have children. He was not ready to settle down and he convinced her she was too early to settle down too.

Nizam and Nina started jogging up the Bukit Shahbandar area, doing their best not to slip on the steps. It was all about acclimatising to the terrain. After a few times working out at Bukit Shahbandar, it was time to see how far they could push themselves. Nizam kept telling himself and Nina that this was the time to find and break their limits.

To push themselves harder, Nizam and Nina would listen to upbeat music with their earphones on. The idea was to drown out any negative thoughts about giving in to their fatigue.

One fine afternoon, Nizam and Nina went to Bukit Shahbandar Forest Recreational Park and started their grueling run up and down the hills. They had started out running up in tandem, but Nina was distracted in her thoughts, more than usual. She had a secret she could not tell her husband. She tried her best to keep up with Nizam but always ended up several steps behind him. Heaving and constantly wiping beads of sweat from her eyes, she felt very saddened by the fact that Nizam never looked back to check on her. He was always in his own world, separate from hers. The loud upbeat music she was listening to did little to stop her from drowning in her own anguish. She had hoped Nizam would take a breather, spend time to enjoy the hill view and chat with her.

Midway through the course, Nina nearly tripped. She managed to avoid from hitting her head on to a small rock on the ground. Cursing out loudly, she saw one of her shoelaces had come undone. She looked up and saw her husband still running uphill and not stopping. She quickly tied up her shoelaces and sprinted as fast as she could. Jumping up a few steps at a time; rage fueled her. She was furious that she could have hit her head and gotten knocked unconscious and he would not have noticed. She could not believe that she was married to this uncaring selfish man, whose apparent 'quality' was vanity. She pushed herself harder, pushed through the pain. Nina might even slap him hard. She was definitely going to have a fight with him there in Bukit Shahbandar. She was going to shout at him and tell him she's had enough.

No matter how much harder she pushed herself, she could not catch up to Nizam. He seemed to have picked up speed too. When they were about to reach one of the peaks, she let out her frustration and shouted as loudly as she could, cursing him for being an uncaring husband. She had hoped he would stop, but he did not. She saw him continue running up towards the peak, as she sobbed uncontrollably. Wiping her tears, she started to notice her husband was continuing to run above the peak, which she thought was impossible unless there was an invisible stairway to the sky. He ran higher up and until it was very clear he was running on nothing but air.

'How could he run high up into the sky?' She started to panic. When she came to the conclusion that it was not her husband but some form of ghost that was pretending to be her husband, the sky quickly turned gray and everything grew dark around her.

Hyperventilating, she tried to find her way down, but there was now more than one trail down. All of the trails looked the same, which was impossible as there was only one track at this point. She could see hundreds of shadows lurking in the trees; hundreds of evil eyes staring at her, piercing through her soul.

Nina bit herself as she huddled to protect herself. There was an ear-piercing cackling from the tall trees around her. She could feel a Presence that was heading towards her. She did not know where to run. This was the end for her, right here, right now. She started to recite 'Ayat Kursi' to protect herself from evil spirits and then prayed loudly for protection from God, not just for herself but for the unborn child she was carrying.

Heavy footsteps approached her, she dared not look. She had no means of protecting herself. She was in prime fitness and now she was pregnant. A wet cold hand grabbed her right arm. Nina screamed out in terror, kicking the ground to push herself away from 'the arm'. Seeing her actions were futile, she looked up to meet the 'face of Death'. Instead she saw 'its' eyes, gentle and confused - it barely had a humanoid shape, its mist-like figure was almost drifting in the air. The apparition waved to Nina and pointed to a direction. With no words spoken, Nina knew it would not harm her, Nina knew it would help her. The other trails disappeared and there was now only one track down. Nina walked down slowly and carefully, whilst maintaining eyesight with the gentle spirit. Soon enough, she had walked a distance down and could no longer see the spirit.

She recited Holy Verses as she slowly walked down the steps all the way to the car park. By the time she got there, it was already dark. Her husband Nizam had been waiting impatiently by the car, demanding to know where she went. She refused to talk to him.

When she got home, she packed up her things and left him without saying a single word. She stayed with her parents and remained separated from Nizam. Nizam believed that his wife was somehow possessed. Nina told him nothing. She thought he would never understand. After she gave birth to a beautiful daughter, she divorced her husband. Since then, she had gained weight and is no longer a fitness enthusiast. She had remarried to a patient of mine who is definitely rotund. However, I have noticed Nina is much happier now these days.

The Attack

Names have been changed to protect identities.

More than 30 years ago, a soldier had gone missing in the jungles of Labi. He was missing for 23 days during a military training exercise. The Search and Rescue (SAR) mission was stopped after 14 days, as there were no traces found of the missing soldier. On the 23rd day, he was found under a house in a rural village in the next district i.e. Tutong. I found out about this incident from my patients, friends and clinic staff. One of my friends, Kyle was a 'ranger' i.e. member of the Special Task Platoon (STP). I found out there were other strange and unexplained happenings during that SAR mission.

***

Captain Sarin did not sleep well during the first week of the SAR mission in Labi. There had been several encounters including the mysterious soldier (check the first book - chapter Not One of Us) who could not infiltrate the forward base camp because they had a protection spell around it. This spell is called a guris, and had been set up by one of the civilian 'specialists'. One of Captain Sarin's men kept calling them that. Essentially, they were self-proclaimed experts in the spiritual world. A number of them were actually scamsters and conmen whilst others were 'white-hat' magicians and healers. One or two of them were unfortunately black magic practitioners. Yes, someone coined the term 'black-hat magicians'! Other than Captain Sarin's unit, there were other soldiers there: the 'regulars'. Most of these soldiers had been assigned to provide support and logistics as well as to search nearby sectors of the jungle.

Captain Sarin and his platoon had covered and searched their designated quadrant for the day and found nothing. No footprints and clues that would lead to the missing soldier. The tropical heat and the terrain was unforgiving. His platoon had been doing this for years and yet it was not something anyone could get too accustomed to.

After a short debriefing with the commanding officer at the base camp, Captain Sarin and his men prepared for an early night. They would have to wake up very early in the morning and search in a new sector.

Captain Sarin was woken up by shouting and probing flashlights. It sounded like they were under attack! His men and himself jumped up and ran towards the source of the commotion. They could see faint beams of lights pointing towards the sky. Sarin's men switched on their flashlights and searched the night sky. There was a figure of a man dangling upside down in thin air. It was one of the soldiers, screaming for help whilst struggling to get hold on to anything. There was nothing there but the thin air. The soldier was swung from one side to another, as though being toyed. One of the civilian specialists recited a prayer and eventually the soldier flew to one end of the base camp, hitting a tall tree and then slowly falling, but not before hitting the branches down the way.

The civilian specialist told Sarin that it seemed the jungle spirits had attacked from above. They must have leaned from one of the large branches of the towering jungle trees to overcome the protection of the guris.

"We have to rescue that soldier now!" Captain Sarin pointed at the soldier who had landed outside the base camp. The jungle was pitch-black and what had happened shook most of the soldiers. Hence, no one volunteered. It was up to Captain Sarin and his platoon. Sarin looked at his watch, it was now 1am. Ghost or not, a brethren is in need and he may be badly injured too.

Gosni, the civilian specialist or spiritual master, advised Sarin to take precautions and to trust his instincts. They could not do anything about the flaw in the guris. A dome-shaped guris spell would be set up once it was daylight. In the meantime, everyone in the base camp was vulnerable.

Whilst Sarin and his men rushed to find the injured soldier, the other soldiers in the base camp organised themselves in groups and prepared themselves against an impending attack from an invisible enemy.

Captain Sarin and his men slung their semi-automatic rifles behind them as they ran into the dark foliage at great speed; machetes out, poised and ready to slash whatever may come.

The fallen soldier had landed behind one of the larger jungle trees. Its trunk was bigger than a family-sized car. Sarin and his men cautiously went around the trunk to reach the other side. It seemed like forever to reach the other side. The night air grew thick as they anticipated an attack from the jungle spirit attacker.

On the other side of the trunk laid the wounded soldier, groaning and writhing in pain. Broken branches and leaves were strewn all around him and under him. The tree branches must have broken his fall. Sarin deliberately shone the flashlight at his face. The soldier squinted and covered his eyes from the blinding light. He had badly injured his leg and his shoulder.

"Can you stand up?" one of Sarin's men asked him. The wounded man tried to but could not even sit up, let alone stand up.

"In that case, we will carry you."

Captain Sarin felt uneasy. Something was wrong. He put his hand in front of his men and told them not to move closer to the wounded soldier.

"Before we do that, I want you to recite to us the three Qul Verses!"

The wounded soldier immediately jumped on his feet, grinned slyly and then yelled out, "Never!"

Sarin thought to recite the three important and simple Verses from the Holy Quran would be the best test and unfortunately, he was right. The eyes of the wounded soldier rolled up and he collapsed back onto the pile of broken branches and leaves.

Sarin felt cold air rush out from the wounded soldier, and then an unseen force push against him.

"Carry that soldier back to the base camp!" Sarin ordered his men, whilst gesturing he would stay behind to fend off the mystical enemy. His machete was poised high up, and ready to strike.

As the distance grew between Sarin and his men, Sarin felt he was surrounded by a Presence. He thought he heard movement from one corner, he responded by facing the perceived direction of the enemy. Sarin took cautious steps backwards towards the base camp.

All alone in the pitch-black darkness, he could hear a faint laughter, which seemed to be moving around him. He gripped the wooden handle of his machete so hard, he could barely feel his fingers.

Sarin heard faint movement. Suddenly, by pure instinct, he felt a sudden movement heading towards him. Without a sound, a dark shadowy figure leapt towards him.

Sarin dodged the attack and slashed at the shadow. The machete sliced through the shadow. It felt like cutting through thin air, yet it was not mere air. Growling in pain, the shadow struck back at Sarin. Like hot blades stuck inside his tummy, the surge of pain was so overwhelming that Sarin dropped his machete. Sarin fell to the ground writhing, barely able to breathe. He could see his attacker; a dark shadow standing next to him. Sarin wondered if he was going to be dealt a deathblow.

He heard his name being called out, and a set of heavy footsteps heading towards him. The shadow disappeared quickly.

One of his men; a Dusun tribesman, had came back for him. He carried Sarin over his shoulders and ran back towards the base camp.

Sarin was in constant pain. There were 3 small but distinct bruise-like spots on the left flank side of his abdomen. Otherwise there were no wounds.

He did his best to continue with his mission, fighting through the pain. Sarin did not have any other encounters, especially after Gosni performed a protection ritual on him.

Gosni did his best to heal the spiritual wound, and reduce Sarin's pain.

When the mission was stopped and wrapped up on day 14, Sarin went to see the army doctors. He had also gone to see other civilian doctors but no one could figure out the cause of his pain. They could not find anything wrong with him. Sarin gave up after one physician suggested that he should see a psychologist.

He also tried 'ber-ubat kampung' which was basically traditional medicine and spiritual healers. The only thing that had happened was that he was spending more but the pain was not getting better.

Luckily, one of his good friends suggested an uncle who was versed with matters of spiritual healing. That uncle, an elderly holy-man told Sarin that the only way he could treat the wound was to heal his soul. Sarin had to find his way to better himself and begin the search for God and His Peace. This was attained through prayers and deep meditation. Sarin had to let go of his previous life and begin a new simpler and righteous life.

With time, the pain had disappeared completely but the 3 spotted marks on the left side of his abdomen remain to this day.

The Welcome

Wilhelm Bayona, who is known as Mr. M, is an outgoing person. He loves making new friends and helping others in need. He is an Anime fan and is a model kit collector. He was a choir singer and acted in theatre during his college days. He now spends his time thinking of ways to conquer the universe (in a fun and crazy way) before he retires. He currently works at the Mabohai shopping complex where he manages the property. He is also an active writer.

It has been more than 20 years since I first arrived in Brunei. I had taken the only available flight from Manila and arrived in Brunei late in the night. It was an exciting time and I felt a great sense of hopeful opportunities.

My newly-met colleagues had shown me around my new residence. Initially, I was impressed with my new home. The building was a three-storey flat, with each floor having two apartments. In each apartment, there were 3 beds in the sleeping quarters, one for each member of my team. My apartment was on the third floor, which meant I would have a better view of the surroundings.

I met up with my housemates who welcomed me with embraces. We had shared pleasantries but since it was already late, we kept things short and sweet. I was keen to settle in for the night and wake up fresh and ready for a brand new day.

However, on my first night in Brunei, I had difficulty falling asleep. I wondered if I had drank too much coffee during the day, or if I had accidentally drank coffee on the plane. I was pretty sure I was caffeine-free. I concluded that it must be due to the excitement of a new place coupled with home sickness. I was never used to sleeping in a new place with unfamiliar surroundings. And yet, in spite of all my reasonings, I wondered if it was something else. Perhaps there was something odd about my surroundings. I couldn't put my finger on it. Eventually, I did fall asleep.

On the second night, having such a long day, I decided to call it a night at around 7pm. I was the only one in the apartment. With no one to talk to, I fell asleep easily. However, I was woken up by loud knocking on the door to our flat. I looked at my watch and groaned. It was around 9 pm - which meant I had only slept for 2 hours. The knocking on the door continued, growing louder and louder. Did one of the staff forget his keys? I thought they told me they wouldn't be back till 11pm. Perhaps they had been given an early break. The knocking on the door continued, so I hastened to the door.

However, when I went to open the door, there was no one there. I wondered if they had given up or gone elsewhere. I checked the staircase but there was no one running or walking up or down. I decided to check and went down to the second floor just to see if there was anyone there. The stairwell was empty.

I should have been annoyed but I began to have goosebumps all over. There was an eerie feeling in the air. It was then that my mind started to worry if I would be locked out of the flat and be left out. I hurried back to my flat and to my relief the door was still ajar.

The next few days were followed by equally eerie disturbances. The knocks on the door happened even during the daytime, usually after 5 pm. The strange thing was that it would always be three loud knocks, the intervals were the same, no variations. I figured that if it was a child or someone playing a prank, then the knocking would not be that consistent. As always, when I opened the door to check it out, there would be nobody there. And yet I felt someone was watching me.

I also began to notice that after 7 pm onwards, I would hear footsteps in the living room area heading towards the hallway and then to the bedroom. The sound of footsteps would sometimes be fast as though running, whilst at times the footsteps sounded as though they were slow, steady steps. I noted the direction was always consistent – it would start from the living room area and then end up in the bedroom area. Who or what was making this sound? I surmised that if the steps were hurried and quick, and sounded light, they belonged to little children. When the steps were heavy, steady and plodding, it belonged to an adult. But where were they? I asked myself if this was a supernatural presence.

One evening, I found out. I was lying face-down in bed, when I felt the room become cold quickly. I did not switch on the air-conditioning. I wondered if it had switched on by itself. Before I could turn over, I suddenly felt a tingling sensation on my lower back. It felt like a small finger running up my spine. The hairs on my neck stood up. I had hoped that was the only thing that would happen. And then, I heard a shrill innocent laughter, a child's laugh.

The sound unmistakably came from under the bed. I did not know what to expect. I mustered my courage and looked over the edge of my bed.

There was a 'child' with shiny black round eyes looking innocently back at me. To say that I was scared would have been natural, but I wanted to meet the spirit. 'He' did not say anything, I did not utter a word. However, I mentally told him to please not bother me again. Without uttering a single world, I told him that he could play, but not to bother me. He disappeared smiling.

After that, the incidents stopped except for one particular night.

That night at around 3am, my flatmates; Henry and Bernie, and I were already asleep in our separate beds. Their beds were adjacent to each other with a small table in between. My bed was perpendicular to theirs. On that table there was a table lamp and a picture frame of Henry's girlfriend.

We were woken up by the sound of violent shaking of the table. We all thought it was an earthquake. After all, we were all from the Philippines, where earthquakes do occur. At first, we were relieved to see that it was only the small table that was shaking. Then, we were bewildered, as the three of us watched the table shake until both the table lamp and the picture frame fell off the table, breaking both items. After regaining composure, I asked the other two if they saw what I had seen and they both answered yes. We decided to go back to sleep as we reassured ourselves that it would not bother us anymore. I thought about the child ghost and his innocent-looking eyes. I knew he would not harm us. I wasn't sure if Henry and Bernie were able to sleep that night, but I slept well.

I eventually moved to a new residence shortly after that. I would never forget my first nights in Brunei especially since that was my first poltergeist encounter in Brunei.

Ride to Kuching

Yusof is a friend of mine who had joined the army after his A-levels instead of pursuing a university degree. He was one of those guys you knew would join the armed forces as he was quite a tough guy and yet had a gentle heart. He was a keen sportsman and excelled during his time as an army cadet. He was quite smart but felt he needed to belong to the 'family' i.e. the armed forces.

Military training was tough and rigorous. Yusof had no issues with it. He rose quickly in the ranks to become an NCO (non-commissioned officer). He was focused on providing his best for his fellow brethren and did not have anything else to think about. He was single and had his youth. However, after his former classmates started graduating, getting on with their careers and then getting married, Yusof started to feel insecure about himself. He tried his best to occupy himself with his military work, as well as improving his fitness level through enduring discipline in physical training.

One day, he was told he had to take a vacation. His commanding officer was worried that Yusof was showing signs of strain. Yusof could not refuse a direct order from his superior. He did not know what to do. He had never been on a holiday before. With no real plan insight, he took his passport, lightly packed a small backpack and then got onto his Kawasaki Ninja sports bike. The neon green motorbike was his pride and joy. The flashy colour was simply his choice, he had no intent of showing off or wooing the girls with it. It was simply his favourite colour. He had no idea where he was going.

He rode fast and hard to the Sungai Tujoh immigration post and then rode on to Miri. Having reached there with ease, he pondered upon if he should chill in Miri or go somewhere else. He had never been beyond Miri. He thought he should ride on until he reached Bintulu. He rested in Miri for a night and then the next day, he made his way to Bintulu.

The roads were not perfect but it was doable. Sometimes, the road had a number of potholes whilst at other times, the road was pebbly or rather the gravel from the asphalt road had gotten very loose.

When he reached Bintulu, he hung around the town and decided on a whim that he would ride on all the way to Kuching. He had never been to Kuching and that was the 'capital' of Sarawak state.

After making several stops on the way to Kuching, he made a bet with himself that he would reach

Kuching that same day, even if he had to ride on through the night.

Whenever he could, he would push his bike to breakneck speed. The loud fast Kawasaki Ninja tore through the Sarawak night. Yusof thought he had done well. He had gone through Sibu and had already passed Sarikei. Kuching city was getting nearer and nearer and yet, it was still a long way to go. Yusof was on a very dark road, flanked with hills and very tall jungle trees, when he hit a large pothole. He was caught by surprise as he heard a loud crack and crumble. He got knocked off his bike and landed on soft grass. He checked himself quickly and was grateful he had no serious injuries. His motorbike had skidded down the road a distance away.

When he eventually got to his bike, he could see the mangled mess the front fork of his poor motorbike had become. This rendered his motorcycle completely useless. He could not even wheel his motorcycle forward. He left the motorcycle hazard lights on and knew he had to hitch a ride from a passing vehicle. It had to be a pickup truck as there was no way he was going to leave his motorcycle there.

There were no cars passing by for a while. The night grew longer and Yusof sighed wearily. In the near distance, he could see a small light heading towards him. It was too dim to be a car or a motorcycle, and it was coming from the roadside. Soon enough, Yusof could see a figure of an old man, pushing his bicycle heading towards him.

Yusof thought it'd better not be a ghost, because he was in no mood to have a haunted experience!

The old man greeted Yusof, and Yusof greeted him back.

"Hey old man, what are you doing here in the middle of the night? You better not be a ghost because I would be extremely unhappy about that!" Yusof raised his voice angrily. He had never seen a ghost and he assumed ghosts had always been afraid of him.

"Calm down son. I am on the way home. You seem a bit troubled, so why don't I just wait here with you - at least until you have calmed down?" said the old man.

"Okay but if you turn into a ghost or do anything funny, I am going to have to punch you!"

The old man laughed, "What's with all the aggression, young man? You have so much to live for. As for your motorbike, it can be fixed in Kuching."

The old man was able to calm Yusof down and they had a deep conversation about life and Yusof's worries about the future. He was quite surprised at how easy it was to open up to this old man.

In the distance, a car with bright lights was approaching them. Yusof mentioned that he was not going to leave his treasured motorcycle there, so he had to hitchhike a truck.

"In that case, I will stay longer, keep you company and protect you," said the old man.

Yusof scoffed at the idea of being protected by this thin frail old man, but appreciated his company.

After that, several cars passed by them. The car lights had lit the road and Yusof noticed someone on the other side of the road. It seemed like an old woman; she was walking up and down the road opposite them.

"Is that your wife or girlfriend, old man?" Yusof laughed. He was about to point his finger towards the old lady, who was dressed in a batik-style sarong dress when the old man smacked his hand down.

"Some things are best left alone. You don't want her to cross the road towards us," the old man warned.

The sound of a pickup truck caught Yusof's attention. He quickly got on his feet and flagged the truck down. The driver of the pickup truck was friendly and was keen to have a driving companion in the middle of the night. They hauled the motorbike onto the back of the truck. Before they drove off, Yusof looked around for the old man but he was not there.

"Did you see the old man who was with me just now?" Yusof asked the driver.

"I did not see you with anyone. It was just you and the motorbike," the driver's voice strained in panic, and he quickly gestured for Yusof to get into the pickup truck quickly. They had to leave that area immediately.

Yusof glanced on the other side of the road. He could see the old woman there. She was no ordinary elderly woman. He could see her putrid face and her menacing red eyes. Yusof felt chilly all over. Neither Yusof nor the driver spoke much on that long drive.

When he arrived in Kuching in the morning, he left his motorcycle at a decent (trusted) workshop. He rented a room at a nearby hotel and suddenly became feverishly ill. It took him several days to fully recover. Every night he could see glimpses of the elderly lady with the rotting face and her mean red eyes. The doctors in Kuching told him he had dengue. Yusof thought he had a brush with Death.

1964

This story was shared by Luqman who; even to this day, is unaware that he is bound by his bitter past, and only he, can choose to set himself free.

It was the year 1964. Luqman was only 14 years old. Yet he was very outgoing and adventurous. He had to be. He had to find any excuse to stay away from home as he had an abusive stepmother, who would beat him frequently and berate him for every little mistake he made. Worst of all, she abused him through food deprivation. She would feed her own children first, and made sure he watched them enjoy their meals, whilst he sat feeling hungry and pitiful. His own father always sided with his stepmother and never believed him. His father was a busy man and was never there. Nobody seemed to care for him. There was no child abuse helpline back then. No one reported child abuse to the police. In 1964, no one wanted to know about child abuse.

Luqman was a very bitter child. His only solace was that he had three close friends: Abu, Salleh and Razali. They shared a commonality: a 'broken' home. Despite the hardship, they tried to have fun. They had to spend as much time away from their homes as possible. In Brunei, all forms of entertainment for children meant going outdoors. It was a time when parents could let their children out and not be worried about when they would come back. This was very true, especially with Luqman and his friends. Somehow, the children acquired their own bicycles. Their bicycles were actually abandoned adult bicycles which they had repaired themselves through guesswork and asking other adults on how to fix bicycles. Their bicycles were everything to them. It was their means of adventure and escape. The four of them cycled everywhere. Unlike now these days, there were not that many cars on the roads. The cars back then were also slow and noisy, which gave ample warning time for the young cyclists.

Luqman and his three friends would often skip school and travel for days. Altogether they had three adult bicycles between them, which meant one person had to take turns sitting on the bicycle back rack, which was not comfortable, unless a small wooden board was tied to it. Sometimes, they would take turns running and racing against the other three who had bicycles. Their adventures and friendship bonded them closer than they were to their own siblings. With their new-found freedom, there was no one telling them what to do and no one stopping them from doing whatever they wanted.

Sometimes, they would camp at certain places, like a jungle, at a rubber plantation, an empty field or even at a hill. Of course, camping did not mean having a tent and sleeping bags. They had none of that luxury. It simply meant sleeping under stars and tolerating all the insect bites, which they had gotten used to anyway.

One day, Luqman and his three friends had cycled all the way to a cliff beach in Berakas. Going downhill with their bicycles, they made their way to the coarse sand beach. After hiding their bicycles in a memorable and distinct shrub, the boys ran to the water. The morning sun was shining brightly and the sea sparkled gold. Without any concern for the dangers of the sea, they swam in the open sea. Later, they caught fish with makeshift fishing lines and hooks.

By late afternoon, they had set up a small fire on the beach and cooked their fish in the open fire. There was nothing tastier than freshly grilled fish. Everyone was lying down near the fire, savoring the aromatic, savory scent of the grilled fish. They were relaxed and eager to start the feast, except for Abu.

Abu, the eldest amongst them, had been acting strangely since their swim. He was always watching over his shoulder and seemed not as sure-footed as he usually was. Luqman asked Abu what was bothering him. Abu said he felt as though they were being watched. Luqman stood up and looked around.

"I don't see anyone here," Luqman shrugged his shoulders.

Abu gestured to everyone to start eating the fish, which was a good way to distract everyone of his thoughts. It was also a good way to distract himself of his uneasiness.

After the fish had been finished and scraped clean to the bones, Abu and Razali volunteered to bury the bones. This was their custom, which they thought would stop rats and other pests from coming near them.

Luqman announced where he was going to sleep, which was near the warm smokeless fire. Everyone else chose a spot next to each other.

They watched the orange sun sink into the black and orange sea. Although they had seen so many sunsets together, every sunset seemed like a new experience for them. The darkness of the night enveloped the landscape and the sea. There was nothing much to do other than watch the stars, talk about their dreams and future life when they become adults, and when they no longer have to face the cruelties at home. There was peace here under the gentle stars and the sound of the waves lapping on to the sandy shore.

However, their conversation was interrupted by a sudden deafening sound, which at first sounded like a hiss and yet it wasn't. They listened intently and realised it was a fizzing sound. Luqman thought it sounded like a giant Coca-Cola soda bottle being opened, except there was no subtle pop at the end, and this sound was very loud.

The four boys got up onto their feet and lit a nearby piece of driftwood into fire to use as a torch. They had no flashlights, and this was the only means of light for them. Their four orange fire torches waved violently in the sea breeze, the only illumination on the beach. The boys cautiously ran towards the sound which was coming from the water. It was so dark that they could not see anything. Abu instinctively threw his torch high up towards the sea. Before the torch hit the water and extinguished itself, the four teenagers could see large bubbles coming from the water surface.

Luqman got closer to the water. He too could see bubbles effervescing from the surface. Razali was the first to suggest that they stay away as far as they could from the beach.

Before anyone could respond, they heard a loud splash followed by a growl. The boys ran away from the water and sprinted towards the dark jungle. The torchbearers gripped their torches hard. To them, this was their light and their weapon. They could hear heavy footsteps from their pursuer, the vibrations shaking their bodies as they tumbled into the jungle. Whatever it was, no one dared to look back. They knew it was a giant demon of some kind. They entered the jungle, not caring about the shrubs and vegetation that made many tiny cuts on their limbs and faces.

Everything in the jungle was uphill from here. As long as they were getting uphill, they would soon clear the jungle and be on the main road which they thought was safe.

Someone suggested they spilt up,. Abu went with Luqman as he had no torch. The two of them ran as fast as they could uphill. Each step up was more of a jump as they scrambled from rock step to another. Pulling onto vines to speed up their ascend, they could feel their pursuer getting closer and closer. They could feel their lives being pulled away from themselves.

It seemed like forever before they could reach the top of the cliff. Abu was the first to reach the top, Luqman threw the torch up on to him so that he could climb to the top. However, he lost his step and fell. Abu jumped down and helped Luqman up.

It was at that very moment the two boys saw a sinister shape in the dark night. It was as tall as the trees, with slender limbs. Frozen in terror, Luqman saw a large claw swoop down onto them. Abu pushed Luqman up and away from the swooping claw. Together they scrambled to the top. The other two boys were already at the top, still holding their torches.

They too could see the giant shadowy demon at the top of the cliff. They had hoped they would be safe here, but there was no such boundary. The four of them kept running on the main road. They ran for their lives, not turning back for a moment until they saw a passing car. Saved by a car, they thought.

The motorcar had stopped, and the driver offered to take them home. It was when they got into the car that they realised one person was missing. Abu was not with them. They were sure Abu was right beside them.

The driver; Mr. Damit, a middle-aged man who knew all the families of the boys helped them to search for their missing friend. He drove near the beach cliff entrance, in the hopes that they would find Abu. Abu was nowhere to be found. However, as much as they wanted to go down the cliff and search for him in the jungle and the beach, Mr. Damit forbade them from doing so. They would have to come back tomorrow to look for Abu.

On the way back, Mr. Damit told them no one goes to that beach especially after dusk. He told them an ancient story about two Kedayan tradesmen.

***

A long time ago, two Kedayan brothers had been carrying a large amount of rice in their 'takiding' (a traditionally weaved backpack). The two brothers had been walking from Terusan and were heading towards their village near the Water Village or Kampong Ayer. They had walked by the beach as they thought it would be easier. There would be no shrubs to cut and no large animals to worry about. They had promised themselves to get there within three days. It was a small race between the two brothers. However, they had carried too much rice and became fatigued. They kept pushing themselves to outdo the other brother. By the time they got to Berakas beach, they collapsed under a large tree, and slept throughout the day and night. In the morning, one brother had woken up and found the other brother had died in his sleep.

He did not have the energy to bury his brother. He left his brother's takiding there and vowed to bury his brother once he got home. However, after returning to the beach with other village men, they found the takiding was still intact and the rice was still there unspoiled but found no corpse of his brother. There were no footprints or signs that the corpse had been moved. Ever since that day, the place seemed to have been cursed.

***

Mr. Damit was surprised that the boys had not heard of that story before.

The boys had made it safely home, only to be severely beaten by their parents. The next day, a search party was formed to find Abu. Abu's body was found face down on the coarse sand beach. Everyone said he must have drowned, and yet his body and his clothes were dry. Abu's family were aghast by the look on his face – it was the face of a boy with a frozen scream. No one asked any questions. Autopsies were never done during those days.

Everyone accepted that it was fated. Everyone had to accept it was fate.

Ever since that day, the three boys rarely went out together. They grew up and in spite of their hardships, they had their own little successes in life. Occasionally when they did meet up, especially in their old age, they would share with each other how they felt Abu's soul was always with them, watching over and protecting them from danger.

Flash

Remember Zul in the previous book? Well after reading this story, you are going to figure out that he is a kind of spiritual magnet.

Zul, who is my mentor's nephew lived near Junjungan village. They had a large house with a very large backyard. The jungle surrounded their house. Their nearest neighbour was a short drive away, but for Zul, it was a good excuse to use his bicycle and cycle to meet up with his neighbours.

His neighbour's children cycled with him. They imagined themselves as a bicycle gang. No, not biker gangs. It was more like geeks on mountain bicycles who raced against each other, by going up the hills nearby. Of course, it was much more fun to go downhill. The roads were flanked with tall jungle trees on both sides, so no matter what time of day or how hot it was, the trees would provide ample shade for them.

One late afternoon, he went over to his neighbour's house but his friends were not around. They had gone to attend a family emergency. Zul had expectations for the day, he wanted to go down the hill with his new upgraded Shimano bicycle gears.

To be precise, he wanted to test and show off his new upgrades. He decided not to cycle home, but instead he would cycle on his own. He knew that one of the advantages of cycling with his friends was so that they could look out for incoming cars. Zul decided that he would not have to worry and he would take extra precautions by being more aware.

A part of him felt uneasy about his decision but this was easily justified by the opportunity to test out his bicycle. It was an opportunity to push it to its limits, though it would be unwitnessed.

Zul pedaled up to the top of the hill. He began to appreciate the splendid view of the surrounding jungles and the houses nearby. He noticed how quickly the clouds had darken on one side of the hill. Whilst he prepped himself for the fast sprint down, he suddenly felt scared. He was sure it wasn't because he was having second thoughts about the ride downhill. Instinctively, he looked behind him, and saw a ghostly female figure dressed in white.

He couldn't make out its face as everything seemed blurred. In reflex, he pushed himself and his bicycle down the hill. He pedaled as fast as he could. He glanced behind him and saw 'she' was chasing him. With that, he got up and pushed the pedals even harder. The wind pushed against his face as he raced past blurred images of the jungle trees. He could hear her loud growl as she moved even faster.

Zul kept glancing back and saw that she was catching up to him. At one point, he looked back and saw the ghost reaching out with her rotting hands to try to catch him. He was barely a hair's breadth away from being caught. His heart pumped harder, as his legs pushed furiously against the pedals. He decided not only would he ride out of the saddle, he would also lean his torso forward, keeping his head lowered onto the actual handle. He figured he would reduce his air resistance and hence go much faster. He had never done this before. But then again, he had never been chased by a ghost before.

It was at this moment the sky began to weep. To make things worse, it rained heavily. He could barely see the pebbled road and yet he could see the ghost that was about to catch him. He had to shake his head from side to side to shake off the rain from his eyes, whilst he gripped tightly on to the bicycle handle.

Zul could see his neighbour's house and he knew he would be safe once he got there. It was at that instant that there was a cold tight grip on his right shoulder. It was too late. She had caught him. Before Zul could do anything, he was blinded by a very bright light. Zul figured this was what happens when people die.

Zul was awaken by the sound of thunder and large rain drops smacking on to his face. He was lying on his back by a shrub near the side of the road. He could see it was otherwise completely dark. He wondered how long he had been lying down there for. He got up and tried to look for his bicycle, but Zul didn't bring a flashlight with him.

As he walked on the road, he suddenly remembered he was being chased by a ghost before he got thrown off the bicycle. In spite of the pain, Zul ran as fast as he could to his own house. His thoughts zoomed in his head as he tried to figure out what had happened. He remembered that she caught him and then there was that blinding bright light.

Once Zul got home, he locked himself in his room, dried himself and immediately went to bed. He didn't want to think about any of that.

The next morning, Zul asked his elder brother to come along with him to look for his bicycle. He told his brother everything that had happened. His brother was skeptical about the event but decided to bring an aluminum softball bat, just in case. They found the bicycle on the side of the road. The bicycle was barely recognizable as its metal tubing chassis was horribly twisted. There were burnt marks on the saddle. His brother reckoned they would not be able to fix his bicycle, and yet carried it up over his shoulders. It was then that they noticed a large black mark in the middle of the pebbled road.

His brother and him did not utter a single word until they reached home. As his brother threw the bicycle into a corner of the garage, he warned Zul never to go up that hill alone.

"I think whatever caught you got struck by lightning. Something divine must have saved you."

Even to this day, Zul wonders what had actually happened.

The Seru

Iswardy Morni is a good friend of mine whom I had first met in Southampton, United Kingdom. He was studying law whilst I was studying medicine at the University of Southampton. He hails from the state of Sarawak in Malaysia. We would usually jokingly remind ourselves that we are both from the same island (Borneo). Other than running successful businesses in the health safety sector, Iswardy continues to be a passionate activist. He is the president of an NGO called Warisan Mayapada Hijau Malaysia, which is dedicated to teaching the poor and disadvantaged segments of society in growing their own food whilst advocating principles of conservation and environmental awareness. Iswardy Morni is also a PKR politician.

We both had a mutual friend named Syed who also studied at the University of Southampton. Unfortunately, Syed passed away at a young age of 25 from heart failure - at least that was what we were told. Iswardy knew Syed way before I did. There was a time when Syed shared with Iswardy about his own supernatural encounter.

It was the year 2003, Syed; aged 15 years, was in a boarding school in Sarawak. Sometimes things can get pretty boring in a boarding school. During these times, Syed would wonder what it would be like to see a ghost with his own eyes. Every time he mentioned his desire, everyone would warn him not to wish for things that he may regret. And yet Syed really wanted to see a ghost with his own eyes or at least an apparition of the ghost. One time, he confessed to his aunt about his desire. His aunt, whom Syed knew was spiritually gifted eventually caved in to his request. She advised him to open the window during 'Maghrib' or dusk and 'Seru' it by chanting certain words to invoke the ghosts. His aunt constantly reminded him to really think about it before doing so. Once a 'Seru' has been done, it cannot be taken back and he might regret his actions.

Syed did not heed to his aunt's warning. All Syed had to do was choose the time and the place. The place had to be at his boarding school dormitory. His dorm had 6 bunk beds which accommodated 12 students. Syed's bed was on the bottom bunk near the middle of the dorm.

Syed waited for his dorm-mates to be away. He did not tell anyone about his plan. He would expect the others to tell him off. During dusk, Syed opened the window of his dorm and performed the 'Seru'. He had expected an immediate result but nothing happened. Syed waited for a few minutes, and yet nothing happened. He waited for half an hour and nothing happened. After waiting for an hour, he got bored. He wondered if his aunt had tricked him. Feeling frustrated Syed decided to go to sleep early.

That night, Syed was woken up early from his sleep. He looked at his watch. It was half past midnight. He realised what had woken him up. It was an eerie feeling of an overwhelming presence. He slowly peeked towards the dormitory door which had been left ajar.

There he could see a dark creepy silhouette of a giant tall figure standing and then slowly walking into his dorm. His dorm was dark but the streetlight outside dimly basked the large room. He could see the figure stoop as it walked into his dorm, its head touching the top of the doorway and the ceiling.

It was at this moment, Syed wondered if it was a bad idea to have performed the 'Seru' in the first place. Syed pretended that he was sound asleep, but somehow, he could sense the 'ghost' knew he was still awake. The shadowy figure crept slowly towards him and eventually towered next to his bunk bed. Syed shut his eyes as tightly as he could and did his best to calm his breathing so as to mimic being sound asleep. He could feel a cold sharp claw-like hand pinch his toes. When he did not respond to it, he found himself being pulled towards one end of the bed, to a point his lower leg dangled from the bed. Syed refused to give in. He continued to fake a snore. Eventually, whatever it was had disappeared.

Syed sighed in relief and promised himself not to ever perform the 'Seru' again.

However, the problem with Syed was that he can be ever so forgetful, or just that sometimes he refused to learn from his previous experience.

Soon enough, being unsatisfied of having not seen an apparition face to face, Syed performed the same 'Seru' during the Maghrib time. Nothing had happened immediately. That evening, his juniors decided to hang out in their dorm. They would talk about all kinds of things and jammed a few songs with their guitars. Syed had completely forgotten about the 'Seru'. They were having so much fun 'chilling'. When everyone was tired, the juniors did not go back to their own dorms but instead chose to sleep on the floor. Syed, of course, slept in his own bottom bunk. Syed had slept facing the wall.

That night, he was awoken by a distinct sensation that someone had climbed over and slept right next to his back. He thought it was one of the juniors who had decided to seek the comfort of his bed. He was going to tell that person to go sleep on the floor or get back to his own bunkbed. However, when Syed tried to turn his back to look at who was on the other side, he felt someone was pushing against his back. Syed could not turn around: he was pushed very hard against the wall and it was not letting him go. No matter how hard Syed tried to turn around or push himself against the wall, he found himself trapped. He felt he was in grave danger. Syed suddenly remembered the 'Seru' and started to recite Quranic verses. After that, he managed to turn around. He had hoped to find one or two of the juniors pulling a prank on him, but there was no one beside him in the bunkbed.

That incident truly rattled Syed. He promised himself to never perform such a deviant deed.

The Longhouse

I met a woman named Evon during a sales event. I was doing a book promotion event at a local shopping mall whilst she was helping to promote her insurance company's latest offer. Evon was a very fair-looking woman. Initially, I thought she was Chinese. She turned out to be an Iban from Temburong. She had a good look at my book and decided to share one of her encounters in Temburong.

Evon still lives in Temburong, though now she commutes between Bandar Seri Begawan and Temburong. Before she had graduated and started work, she lived in their family's stilted wooden Iban 'Rumah Panjang' or longhouse.

Her grandparents, parents, uncles and aunts all lived in the same longhouse. She had lived through the transition of using kerosene lanterns to diesel generators and then finally having utility mains electricity. Living there was very communal and helped strengthen the bonds between all relatives. Chores including cooking and cleaning were done together. More importantly, Evon could play together with her siblings and cousins, all the time. The longhouse was facing the jungle, which meant that the entire family would have a splendid view.

As Evon grew older and was in her teens, she would hang out with her female teenage cousins till late evening.

One night, after participating at a community event or 'balai raya' in a nearby village, Evon and two of her cousins arrived home and decided to chat outside their longhouse. The night sky was filled with sparkling stars. The buzz of the evening had got them talking about who they fancied and the usual gossip mill. They lit and smoked their cigarettes whilst they cracked jokes about the people they met at the 'balai raya'. When they wiped the tears of laughter from their eyes and calmed themselves down, they realised someone else was still laughing. The laughter was more like a loud giggle that quickly grew distant and softer.

Immediately, the hair on the back of Evon's neck straightened up, as her cousins and her remained tight-lipped, whilst staring wildly at each other.

Where was that laughter from? Who or what was laughing with them?

Nobody wanted to say what their immediate thoughts were. Nobody wanted to be the one to 'cabul' or jinx everyone else. As much as they tried to not look around, their eyes wandered away from each other and towards the jungle, where the distant giggling ensued.

Evon could not believe what she saw: a lady in white with long black hair jumping from one tree-top to another. She knew immediately what it was. A 'Pontianak' (vampire demon).

Before they could stand up, they saw another pontianak appear. They seemed to be playing a version of tag which involved hopping above the trees! Although none of the pontianaks were looking at them, Evon and her two cousins ran back into the safety of their longhouse. As per understanding, they did not talk about what they saw that night. The plan was to talk about it the next day.

As Evon curled up to sleep with her family, she could hear knocking on the windows at the rear side of the longhouse. This was the side of the longhouse that did not have a walkway or balustrade, the side not facing the jungle. She saw a silhouette at the window, followed by loud giggling. Whatever it was, it must have been floating in midair to reach to that window. Evon was so scared, she broke out in cold sweat. She was soaking in so much sweat that her clothes were clinging to her body.

It kept knocking on a few of the windows before her father and her uncles woke up and decided to go out with their machetes. One of the elder aunties told them not to bother. She told them it was not worth the effort. This auntie mentioned something about the pontianaks just wanting to 'play'. She chanted loudly a mantra and after she was finished, she told everyone to sleep and to ignore whatever they hear. The giggling outside the longhouse did not last long. Regardless, Evon continued to shiver in fear and she could not sleep until dawn.

The next day, Evon and her cousins were told to help her aunts and mother to prepare Kembayau (also known as Dabai) and other dishes. The elder aunt decided to tell them that many years ago, their youngest aunt had given birth to a stillborn baby girl. The youngest aunt did not last long and died the next day. The elder aunt told them that the pontianaks that they saw were probably the spirits of their youngest aunt and her daughter. As much as it was possible that the pontianaks wanted to play, it was not worth the risk.

Of interest, Evon mentioned to me that the exact term that her aunt used was not Pontianaks but actually Pontianak (mother) and 'Tiyanak' (child).

Best Friends Forever

I knew Mrs. Z as she was my former Maths teacher in college. She decided to share this story with me after reading the first ghost stories book.

Many years ago, Mrs. Z, her husband and her daughter Fifi were living at her parents' house in Panchor Papan village, Tutong. It was the good years when her daughter was closer to her grandparents.

Mrs. Z began noticing that her 2-year-old daughter was always talking and playing by herself. At least that was what it seemed like. Mrs. Z thought what wonderful imagination children have. From the conversations her daughter had with herself, Mrs. Z could figure out that her daughter had two imaginary friends. A boy and a girl. The boy was named Kavalec and the girl was named Jerry. Both were the same age as her.

Sometimes, she would introduce her best friends to guests who turned up to the house. Not surprisingly, none of the guests could see her best friends. Sometimes, she would point them out but there was nothing there but thin air. It was very amusing to most people. For others, it raised the hairs on the back of their necks and arms every time Fifi talked about her imaginary friends.

Mrs. Z had expected that as her daughter grew older, her imaginary play friends would disappear. However they didn't. Soon enough, Fifi was old enough to go to school. Fifi wasn't interested in going to school. In fact, most days, she didn't want to go to school. Her excuse was that she wanted to play with her friends. They didn't want to be away from her either, apparently.

Eventually, Mrs Z moved to an apartment flat in the Capital, where she and her husband could commute easily to work. She had expected her daughter to no longer have her imaginary friends. However, Fifi would mention that they would visit her on certain days. She would usually give advance notice that she would not go to school on certain days as her friends were coming over. For example, if she said her friends were going to come around on Tuesday, then on that Tuesday, she would say she would not go to school!

Neither Mrs. Z nor her husband could cajole Fifi to go to school. She seemed resistant to her father's scolding and idle threats. It was as if the friends were next to her advising how to react to her father's anger. There were times Fifi would say that she already knew what 'Babah's plans were and that this was not real anger coming from her dad! Once her dad got very upset, he locked her in a dark storeroom for several minutes. Fifi was not at all scared. On the contrary, she was amused and didn't shed a single tear. She kept saying that she wasn't afraid in the dark storeroom because her friends had brought their own lights inside the storeroom!

As for school, in the beginning, her teacher didn't seem to be bothered by Fifi's behaviour. There was no harm in having imaginary friends. Soon enough, Fifi interacted less and less with the rest of her class. She didn't pay much attention in school. She seemed busy talking and playing with her imaginary friends.

On days when these friends came around, she hardly ate. Fifi was always busy with her invisible friends. Mrs Z and her husband would constantly worry about what to do with their daughter.

One evening, during a family function, Mrs. Z's brother-in-law's father noticed peculiarities with Fifi and found out the whole story. He advised Mrs. Z to bring Fifi to a spiritual healer - or 'berubat'. He mentioned that he knew she must be playing with 'Bunian' children. 'Bunians' are also referred to as 'Orang Halus' or the invisible people.

Mrs. Z and her husband brought Fifi to a spiritual healer in Lambak village. The 'bomoh' or spiritual healer mentioned that Fifi had been marked by the Bunians. He pointed to a strange black mark on the sole of her left foot. The spiritual healer confirmed that she was indeed playing with two Bunian children. He would describe the children, complete with their names and detailed descriptions. He mentioned that Kavalec was a playful boy whilst Jerry was a girl with long hair and had a face that was very similar to Fifi. On hearing that, Mrs. Z was so spooked. The next day, she brought her daughter to a hair saloon and had Fifi's hair cut very short.

After seeing the spiritual healer, Kavalec and Jerry didn't disappear immediately. They would still come around but the 'visits' and playtime were less frequent. Fifi would be unwell with a high fever when the Bunian children came around. She would also be disinterested in eating or going to school.

Mrs. Z brought her daughter a few times to the spiritual healer and eventually, Kavalec and Jerry disappeared completely from Fifi's life. Life became as normal as it should be with Fifi and her family.

Today, Fifi has been happily married for the past five years. She mentioned she believes Kavalec is still around with her. She cannot see him but those who are gifted can see the 'man' who is always with her.

Interestingly, I did not realize I was already well acquainted with Mrs Z's sister, until I met her during my book event. Mrs. Z's sister, like myself, is also a family physician. I told her I was writing the story about her niece and she knew immediately what I was talking about.

Tear in the Fabric

Dr. Zara is not just a family physician colleague but she was also my mentor in Brunei. We share many common interests and values. She is a fellow writer and in many ways, we are both activists. I was quite saddened when she decided to leave Brunei and work in England, and yet I acknowledged it was very much a necessity for her. Recently she came back to Brunei and she messaged me to meet up. We would talk about everything under the sun, but not before I complained about her one line responses to my emails. When I told her I was writing this second ghost story book, I suddenly remembered she had told me about her supernatural experience in one of the government health clinics in Sungai Hanching.

One afternoon in February 2013, Dr. Zara was finishing off work. She had just finished seeing her last patient and was jotting down her patients' notes when she was suddenly overwhelmed by a strange unexplained sensation. She could feel as though everything in the room had slowed down. Dr. Zara stood up and immediately tried to walk out of her room. Her steps slowed down to almost a standstill and it was much harder for her to breath. The air turned cold and her head grew heavier and heavier. She could feel herself being worn down quickly, becoming groggy. She was not going to fight the feeling anymore and had made up her mind to lay down and sleep on the floor! It was at this moment, an ear-piercing scream shattered her drowsiness. Dr. Zara jumped on to her feet and immediately rushed to the source of the scream.

In the pantry room, which is on the same floor, a nurse curled up against the wall, all shook and crying. A healthcare assistant had also arrived to help with the situation, whatever the situation was. The nurse was hysterical and she had to be carried out of the room. When she eventually calmed down, Zara asked what had happened.

The nurse had been adjusting her headscarf on a wall mirror, which happened to be placed parallel to a smaller mirror on the other side of the wall. The whole idea of the placement of the mirrors was so that you could check your front and back at the same time, by simply looking at the reflection of the mirror in the front mirror. The staff would usually pat themselves on the back and praise themselves for the ingenuity. However, this time, she had no intention of looking at the other mirror but she saw an oddity in the reflection of the other mirror. She saw a dark figure behind her in the other mirror. When she turned around, there was a dark humanoid figure staring at her from within the other mirror. She quickly covered her eyes and face and curled herself in the corner in fear.

Zara did her best to reassure the frightened nurse that it was probably a trick of the mind, as a shivering chill went down Zara's spine. Zara did her best to appear composed and calm, lying through her teeth and doing her best to calm the nurse down and the concerned healthcare assistant.

"You've had a long day. It's best not to talk about it and just go home. The eyes can play funny tricks when we are tired."

The other staff gave Zara a disapproving look. No one wanted to be patronised yet Zara believed it was important not to cause panic. Zara could not explain what had happened to her but this was not the right time to start causing fear and panic in a health center. Being responsible for the clinic, she became aware that incident was not the only supernatural event that had occurred. Throughout the weeks of February 2013, some of the staff began to see glimpses of a lady dressed in white who would appear and then disappear. This occurred during the daytime instead of the expected night time for poltergeist sightings. The staff would not dare remain in a room on their own. They would work in pairs. They even went to the toilets in pairs. The other doctors had also noticed strange sightings especially during lunchtime. Some mentioned the room would suddenly become cold and they would feel as though they were being watched by a dark presence. It was very unnerving. Others swore that they could see; in the corner of their eyes, a white shadow pass by in the corridors of the clinic.

Zara thought this was quite unnerving and disruptive. She confided with a senior colleague who suggested they seek the services of a 'licensed' spiritualist to 'cleanse' the clinic. I remember the time when Zara told me about what had happened. I could not laugh at the irony of things. Of course, Zara was worried about the serious implications with the public that could easily run amok in panic and fear.

After the cleansing rituals, the sightings did not disappear. Zara told me the sightings disappeared that same month after the body of a Malaysian Chinese lady was found by police. Her decomposed corpse had been encased in cement in a house in Salambigar - an adjacent village. This discovery became a national headline news - which also made its way to regional news.

Zara was not entirely sure if it was really related but she found the causality strange. The sightings and incidences stopped abruptly the moment the dead lady's body was found, in the cement block in her friend's garden. Zara wondered if the events surrounding her death had caused a tear in the 'spiritual world fabric' that kept the Unseen from us humans.

Do check out: http://bit.ly/2T7Zk77

Mount Singai

One of my friends in Kuching had alerted me to the events unfolding in Sarawak in September 2018. A 22-year-old man, who was her husband's friend's employee had been hiking up Mount Singai near Bau Town on his own and had been missing for a couple of days. Social media was abuzz with the search for the missing hiker.

Sam (not his real name) a 22-year-old man had meant to hike up the hill with his friend, Adam, on the 17th September 2018. The plan was to meet up with Adam at the main car park at Mount Singai around 8am. However, Sam had met a very beautiful woman who looked like a 'Princess' earlier. The woman had given him flowers and gestured for him to follow her. He was so mesmerised by her that he followed her without question into the jungle of Mount Singai.

Meanwhile, his friend Adam waited for Sam at the carpark. After waiting for a while, Adam had sensed something was wrong. Adam could see Sam's car in the parking lot. He could see footprints that suggested that Sam had gone uphill on his own. Why would he go and do a solo hike ascend? They were supposed to go together. Adam rang his phone. Although mobile phone reception was not amazing, Sam's phone was ringing but no one was picking up. Sam did not respond to any of the WeChat or WhatsApp messages.

Adam decided that he could not wait any longer so he called up three of his other friends and they went up the mountain to search for him. They could not find Sam. It was like he disappeared into thin air.

By 10am, they noticed Sam had updated his WeChat status. There was nothing specific and it did not show any details. Regardless of that, no matter what else they tried, Sam could not be contacted at all.

By 4pm, Adam and his friends reassessed their situation. They knew they could not proceed any further in the tropical jungle mountain. Eerily enough, Adam and his friends began to feel as though they were being watched. It was time to call for help. Adam contacted the Fire Department at 4.30pm and they initiated an official Search and Rescue (SAR) mission.

The Fire department's SAR team started searching at the Catholic Memorial & Pilgrimage Center at Mount Singai. They had hoped that it would be the one place that Sam would go to. However, he was not there. Then they searched the gravel-dirt footpath all the way to the summit. Sam was nowhere to be found.

As time passed by, everyone started realising that this was not going to be a simple search.

The team regrouped and reformulated a new plan. A second SAR operations started at 8.45pm, which covered an area of 50 meters radius around and down the summit, as well as the surrounding area of the footpath. There was no sign of Sam.

Sam's family was also involved in the search parties. They had alerted the whole of Sarawak through the use of social media and volunteers started to pour in. Everyone wanted to find Sam safe and alive.

By this time, Sam had already been missing for more than 24 hours.

Following advice from family, friends and well-intended villagers, Sam's family decided to seek the services of 'Bomohs' or local shamans. They kept pointing to the same spot deep in the jungle, which was near the river. They told Sam's family that Sam was still alive but the jungle spirits were keeping him.

Over the next few days, the SAR mission had involved over 300 personnel which included various hiking groups and teams, paranormal enthusiasts, local shamans (pawang), 'Islamic spiritualist or shamans', translators (for the different ethnic groups) as well as various governmental agencies and non-government organizations (NGO). In addition to that, the Ministry of Defence (Malaysia) had mobilised the special unit DRON (Unmanned Aerial Vehicle or UAV special task force) to be involved in the SAR.

By the fifth day, the nation was gripped in anxiety, as hope for many had waned. There was no sign of Sam. Many worried he was already dead. Others speculated that his body would never be found.

Amongst the search parties was a young shamanistic master by the name of Dar. He was from a rural village called Opar.

On that fifth day, Dar had a strange premonition. He knew he had to go to a nearby waterfall. He brought his fellow disciple with him to the waterfall. There he was met by a lady spirit demon. The lady demon had an overwhelming odour of rotting corpse.

The spirit demon told Dar that Sam had been enticed and entrapped by them. The young man asked for Sam to be released but the lady demon refused. Eventually, she was persuaded on one condition - she was to be given a feast and praising as per Bidayuh Gawai day celebration.The young Shamanistic master agreed and told his disciple to tell the other bomohs. Dar went to his village to perform the correct rituals himself whilst others performed the rituals on Mount Singai.

The next day, Dar told the police, fire department and rescue teams that they could stop their SAR operations tomorrow as Sam would be found tomorrow morning.

The SAR team leaders were initially baffled but were happy there was still some optimism within the SAR mission support community.

It was now the sixth day i.e. 23rd September 2018.

A villager from Tanjung Bowang village had heard very soft cries for help whilst going into the jungle. She was concerned and went back home to ask her husband and friend to investigate. The two villagers went up the mountain and explored the area along a stream. Soon enough, at 8.30am, they had found Sam on a steep hill slope, lying on a large rock. He was in bad shape, he was weak and dehydrated. Sam was clad only in his underwear and he had sustained injuries in all four limbs.

The official SAR team was contacted and the team brought him safely out of the jungle. Sam was rushed to the main hospital for immediate treatment.

Sam had told the rescuers that he could hear the rescuers calling out his name, but he had lost the ability to speak! Of note, he was actually found 300 meters away from the Fire Department (SAR) control post!

Sam told them that he had followed the pretty lady Princess into the jungle and into the house, where they feasted over dinner. Sam had thought it was a banquet fit for a king, the food was very delicious. Later, as he stayed longer in the house of the 'Princess', he saw that the food was not what it seemed, it was actually soil and worms. Sam had escaped from the Princess and the house, but ended up lost and injured on his way to find the path back home.

After 6 days of missing in Mount Singai, Sam was very lucky to be found alive.

Forest rangers and designated tour guides often talk about how dangerous the forested mountains of Sarawak are. This terrain is not for solo hikers and inexperienced adventure seekers. These jungles have thick undergrowth and are dense with very tall trees, whilst sharp rocks, slippery cliffs, deep ravines as well as soft soil and erosion-prone slopes make Mount Singai a dangerous place for thrill seekers.

However, local villagers warn that the real dangers comes from the spiritual guardians of the jungle and Mount Singai, who often appear in the form of beautiful men and women, ready to capture those who trespass Mount Singai.

Intruder & The Conspiracy

Senior Nurse SJ was one guy I had not met for a very long time. Our moments when performing CPR (cardiopulmonary resuscitation) or cardiac arrest calls bonded us as though we were brothers in arms. Of course, this could just be how uniformed civilians create their self-images of bravado to boost a deflating morale.

Anyway, I met him again when I decided to work part-time at the Accident & Emergency Department recently. I told him about my book, Real Ghost Stories of Borneo, and pestered him about his personal experience.

He was not very keen to share simply because back then, I used to scoff off any poltergeist encounters of others, and immediately blame drugs, booze, vivid imagination and syphilis. I reassured him that I would respect him and his sharing.

***

It was the year 2001. SJ was a new nurse and he had just been posted to work at the Sungai Liang health clinic in the Belait district.

Since it was far from his (parents') home, he was allocated an apartment at Sungai Liang village. He thought he would use the apartment when he felt too tired to drive back. He did not like the idea of being away from his family. Besides, he enjoyed cooking with his dad. Yes, that's right. His father was the chef of the house.

The apartment building was not that tall but it was the tallest building there back then. This was before the Sungai Liang Industrial Park (SPARK) and the Brunei Methanol Company had been set up. Sungai Liang village was a quiet village, where many of the residents would commute from, to work for the oil and gas companies.

He had moved in for a week, but had only slept over on the first night. The rest of the nights, he drove back to his parents' house in the Brunei-Muara district.

After having to do an extra long shift and to cover another nurse's shift, SJ realised there was no way he could drive home safely. To compound matters, it was already night time and it had started to rain.

He decided he would sleep in the apartment. SJ was feeling nauseous. He wondered if it was his gastric reflux worsening with stress and sleep deprivation. However, when he approached the door of his flat, he could feel a chill pass through him. SJ ignored the sensation and unlocked the door. The apartment was very cold and before he could switch on the lights, SJ felt an overwhelming evil presence in the room.

In reflex, he shielded his head as 'it' attacked him. It was aiming for his head, but ended up clawing his right forearm. The pain awoken SJ's primordial instincts to fight as warm blood dripped down his arm.

SJ ran towards a corner and switched on the lights. There was nothing there. He scanned around the room and saw the place was a mess. The sofa cushions had been torn apart.

"Did a robber attack him?" he asked himself.
SJ ran off to the kitchen. He found a large kitchen knife. He was not going to go down without a fight.

If it had been a burglar, he would already have confronted the person. SJ concluded that it must have been an evil entity of some kind.

SJ walked out of the kitchen as calmly as he could. And there; in the living room, he could see the Presence.

Staring back at him with very large evil eyes, was a small dark 'child'. SJ gripped the knife handle hard, until he was starting to lose sensation in his hand.

He stared back at the 'child' and realised it was not a child. It was a very large jet-black owl or 'bugang'. He thought it was about 2 feet tall and it was huge.

He had never seen an owl as large as this. 'Bugangs' are usually small and have brown feathers. This owl had black feathers with no markings or pattern at all, and the strangest thing was its head. Its head was very round like a child's head.

The bugang stared at him, not moving at all.

SJ wondered how the bird had gotten in. He looked at the balcony and saw the glass sliding doors were ajar. SJ was pretty sure he had never opened the sliding doors.

This was a perfectly logical explanation for everything that had just happened. By right, there was nothing supernatural about this event, except that within himself, SJ felt the dark presence of an evil entity.

SJ whispered out to the bugang;
"If you are good then you can stay for now. If you are not good, please leave now."

The bugang did not respond.

SJ started to recite the Holy Verses. There was heaviness in his chest. He could sense it was coming from the bugang. Sure enough, the bird stood taller and its feathers seemed to puff up making it look more aggressive, as it growled in a low hum.

SJ slowly edged to the sliding doors of the balcony, making sure he remained in full eye contact with the bugang. He pushed the sliding doors all the way, leaving it wide open. He then slowly walked to the kitchen, knife still in hand, now dripping with his blood from his right arm injury. He closed the kitchen door and walked into his bedroom. All whilst remaining in complete eye contact with the bugang. The bugang watched him intently, not leaving him out of sight.

He closed his bedroom door and sighed in relief.

"How did it get into the apartment? I am pretty sure I did not leave the sliding doors open."

SJ took a shower, cleaning the wound on his right forearm. The owl had dug deep into his arm, but he was still good. He managed to bandage his arm. He thought that there was no way he was going to sleep there, and he was not going to deal with the bugang that night. He had an early work shift tomorrow. It would be best if he just left the sliding doors ajar and leave the apartment, surely the bugang would fly away after the rain had gone.

Whilst changing his clothes, he could hear the sound of claws tapping on the wood-tiled floor. He could also hear something else; loud heavy footsteps coming from the living room.

"I don't have time for this..." he shouted out as he pushed the bedroom door, kitchen knife in hand, and rushed off to exit his apartment.

The drive back from Sungai Liang to his parents' house was not easy. SJ had to fight sleepiness by biting hard on to his knuckles, from time to time whilst turning the radio to full blast.

Precariously, he had dozed off for a few seconds a couple of times whilst driving home, only to be awoken by the haunting vision of the large yellow eyes of the bugang. It was like a nightmare that he was worried would become a reality for him.

SJ arrived safely at his parents' home and went straight to bed.

The next day, SJ woke up early and went to work. Luckily, he would have the whole afternoon off. He planned to sort out his 'apartment issue'. He told three of his male nurse friends about his unwanted visitor and they were keen to see it for themselves and help him out. Of course, if the bugang was still there.

After lunch, SJ and his three friends went into the apartment. The sliding doors of the balcony were wide open and yet the large black bugang was still there. Looking at it this time did not change his perspective of the bird. It was the pure essence of evil.

There was nothing cute about it. It seemed awfully strange and it didn't behave like an ordinary owl.

For one, when they slowly approached the bugang, it did not shirk or move away. SJ had hoped that if the four of them walk towards it, then the owl would retreat to the balcony and then fly away. But that did not happen. One of his friends suggested for the other to catch the bird; who in turn, suggested another friend to do so. No one had the courage to grab the huge owl. SJ suggested they do it together but everyone thought it was a bad idea.

The bugang had held its ground and subdued everyone from attempting anything by staring with these large bright penetrating eyes.

SJ decided to call his father and told him what had happened.

"It's not an ordinary bugang. I want you to come back home tonight. Don't stay at that apartment until the bugang has been removed."

SJ could hear his father's worries in his voice. His father called up an elder - a 'spirit consultant' - to take care of the owl.

They waited for the spirit consultant to arrive. He was the local 'orang pandai' who knew everyone in Belait. However, after looking at the bugang and reciting a few Holy Verses, he confessed to SJ and his friends that he could not move the bugang. Moving so would bring harm to himself and his loved ones. The elder mentioned something about the bugang carrying a powerful spirit.

SJ didn't pay much attention after that as he was distracted by the commotion from the crowd of neighbours who had come round to see the bugang.

One of the building tenants, who was not a nurse, offered to help. He was a middle-aged man with deep set eyes and a scruffy long beard. Without any hesitation, he went straight towards the bugang, and was now staring face to face with the huge owl. SJ could see he was whispering something to the owl. A bugang whisperer, SJ thought.

The neighbour, whose name was Ariyan, managed to convince the bugang to perch on to his arm, and then brought the huge owl out of the apartment. It looked tame on his arm, and yet when it stared at SJ and his friends, its menacing eyes pierced through their souls. People would ask how he had managed to tame the owl. Ariyan shrugged and mentioned he didn't know and that it was his first time being near any owl.

SJ's neighbours, who were also nurses, convinced Ariyan to bring the owl to the clinic to show off to their colleagues, whilst SJ spent his time clearing up the excrement and mess left by the bugang. He closed the sliding doors and wedged in a piece of wood, just in case.

SJ informed his father of what had happened. His father was not pleased and advised him to pack his stuff and go home immediately.

When SJ got home, his father embraced him tightly. SJ was not to stay at that apartment again. SJ's father mentioned that it was no ordinary bugang.

His father believed that the bird was a 'pet' of the neighbour, Ariyan. Its large size would suggest that it was 'home-bred' and not flying much. His father theorised that Ariyan was also nurturing a spirit within the bugang, and the fact he pretended to not know anything about the bugang would mean he was hiding a deeper secret. His father wondered if SJ was a practice target for the bugang and its demon.

SJ applied to be transferred to another clinic. Over the next few weeks, he would see shadows lurking in the corner, especially when he was alone, and worse of all, he was constantly badgered by the feeling that he was being watched.

Being a medical person, he always wondered if this was a trick of the mind. He wondered if the bugang attack and the whole incident had just made him paranoid.

After leaving Sungai Liang and Seria area, he met a few of his old friends and he confided with them about what had happened. They in turn revealed their own experiences in the very same apartment. Some of them had seen the bugang inside the apartment, again not knowing how it got in - this time the sliding doors were definitely closed - they had seen strange happenings, including seeing 'large shadows hovering over their bedroom windows.'

They all came to the same conclusion that Ariyan was a black magician who was practising his dark arts, and he was training his vessel, the bugang.

Left Behind

A nurse friend of mine told me that when the private clinic had just moved to the new location (not disclosed), the staff had noticed strange happenings. The excitement of moving to a new place made everyone ignore the signs. However, the incidences became more frequent and harder to ignore.

The first time it happened was during lunchtime. Usually, the staff nurses; Yuna, Siti and Nurul would stay back. They would have their packed food and eat together during lunchtime when the clinic was closed. They would share stories and laugh at jokes together. It was their own little place and their own little moment.

Lunchtime was nearly over and it was time to clean up. The toilet was at the back of the clinic. To get to the toilet, you had to pass by three rooms, the first was the doctor's office, then the treatment room and last, was the ultrasound room, where the sonographist; Lydia, would perform ultrasound scans on pregnant mothers. The ultrasound room was dark, as Lydia would usually prefer dimmer lighting whilst performing her ultrasound examinations.

Yuna headed towards the toilet, and as she passed by the ultrasound room, she saw Lydia standing there, smiling and not saying a word.

"Lydia, I see you had a bit of an early lunch break. Got to use the toilet, talk to you later!"

After Yuna came out from the toilet, she peeked into the ultrasound room but Lydia was not there. She felt the room was colder than usual, and made a mental note to remind everyone not to set the temperature of the air-conditioning too low.

Yuna walked to the front of the clinic where Siti and Nurul were and asked where Lydia was. The two of them shrugged, "It's Monday today, Lydia doesn't work on Monday afternoons."

"I am pretty sure I saw her just now!"

Yuna could not help from being puzzled by what had happened. It definitely must have been Lydia that she had seen. Though now that she thought about it, Lydia did look a bit fairer than usual and her smile seemed different. Yuna felt a chill pass through her spine and decided not to share with the others what had happened.

On a different day, Nurul, who was always the first to arrive at the clinic had noticed the doctor was already there. Doctor Jay was sitting in her room and looking vacantly at a book. Nurul carried on with cleaning the clinic and getting everything ready before opening time. Thirty minutes later, the other two staff arrived. Nurul told them that Doctor Jay was unusually early today. Without saying a single word, all three of them knocked on the doctor's office but there was no answer. Yuna opened the door and found the doctor's office empty. No one said a single word.

Doctor Jay arrived. She looked as jovial as usual. Nurul asked her if she had turned up to the clinic earlier.

"No, I was having a big breakfast with my children at the new place in town. Why do you ask?"

"Nothing, don't worry about it, Doctor Jay."

Yuna, Siti and Nurul chose to remain tight-lipped about the incident. Nobody wanted to ask the other about what they thought had happened. By the end of the working day, Siti couldn't stand it anymore and confessed that she had been noticing people appearing where they shouldn't have been! 'Gimbaran' as the people would say.

There had been many such incidences with Siti. One time, she thought she saw Nurul in the treatment room and yet Nurul was in the reception area, which would have been impossible without passing by Siti.

Yuna decided to call her aunt, who was an 'orang pandai'. Yuna thought it was best for her aunt to come around to see the place and perhaps carry out a cleansing ritual. However, her aunt was reluctant to come around; she had a relative's wedding to help with. Instead, her aunt asked Yuna to describe what the clinic looked like on the outside. Within a few minutes, her aunt mentioned she could see the clinic, describing some of the decorative ornaments on the wall - her aunt had never been to the clinic before! Eventually, she asked Yuna to look at the fixtures at the four corners of the clinic.

"There's something that doesn't belong to you. Left behind. The owner must have forgotten to take them with him before he left the place."

With no further explanation, her aunt hung up. It was nearly 6pm. The three of them debated on whether they should search for it now or wait till tomorrow. Yuna persuaded everyone to muster their courage and complete the task at hand immediately.

They went to one corner of the clinic building and saw an odd corner fixture at the top. It was not part of the building, and it was not part of the renovation. It must have belonged to the previous tenant. Yuna saw the fixture was actually a small wooden shelf no bigger than her palm. It had been covered with plywood so as not to reveal its contents. Using a ladder, Yuna climbed up and slowly, pried open the wooden fixture. Everyone feared a beast or a demon would be released from it. At this moment, they were so scared that even a small spider would have caused them to shriek hysterically.

Placed carefully in the fixture was a small sealed glass bottle with light brown liquid. Yuna brought it down for the others to see. There was something else inside the bottle. Lifting it towards a lightbulb, they could see a partially rolled piece of light white-yellow cloth with some faded scripture written on it.

"This must be it!" Nurul blurted out loudly.

They found the other wooden fixtures in the other three corners of the clinic. Each had the exact item - though the scripture looked different from each other. None of the women could tell what scripture it was. It definitely did not look Arabic.

They carefully placed the tiny glass bottles in a small padded box and clutching the box for dear life; in case the box dropped accidentally and the contents - whatever it was - was released. They drove hurriedly to the previous tenant's shop. The previous tenant who was an Indian man, at first greeted them happily. However, when Yuna explained to him that they had to return something of his and then showed him the bottles, he looked surprised and then solemn. He apologised to the ladies for their troubles and told them not to ever mention this to anyone. The three women left hurriedly.

After that day, there were no further disturbances in the clinic. From time to time, the three of them would wonder what was exactly inside the bottles and what was the purpose of it. Sometimes they wonder if it was a 'penarik', meant to lure customers to the shop. At times, they wonder if it was a protector, meant to stop thieves and alike from entering the premise. Whatever it was and its purpose, it is now back with its owner. He can reap whatever benefits it provides and pay whatever price 'it' demands from him.

Fisherman's Tale

Bob has been a mentor to me for many years, providing me with useful life advice. You can say he is the doctor's doctor. I would go to his house at night, though at other times, we would go to a swimming pool. In between laps, we would talk about life and our observations.

I would also share with him about my interests which included snorkeling. I was keen to bring him to Pelong rocks and the other snorkeling spots, but he was always wary of going out to sea. One day, he told me about the 'beings' at sea. He told me the 'beings' at sea were far stronger than those in the jungle. He shared with me a story of many of the sea 'people'.

Ali was an old childhood friend of Bob. One day, Bob had business with Ali and had to visit his house. Bob noticed a sleek fibreglass boat in the garage, with beautiful Yamaha engines. It looked new but the long grass had been growing by the trailer wheels. This meant it had not been used much.

After the business deal discussion with Ali, Bob asked about the boat and commented how the boat was in excellent condition. He thought it looked almost new and that it didn't look like it had been used much. Bob was wondering if it was for sale. Ali abruptly stood up and angrily pointed at Bob. He could see that Ali was holding himself back from screaming at Bob. Ali took a few steps back and then walked away to another room, leaving Bob puzzled. Bob wondered if he should leave and come back next time, but he didn't want to leave on a bad note. Besides, he had been served this cup of hot delicious creamy tea or 'teh tarik'- it was a shame to let it go to waste.

Ali calmed himself down and apologised for his outburst. He told Bob that he had only used the boat once, and had not dared to bring it out to sea again.

"Only once?"

Ali shared the story of his first and only fishing trip.

***

Ali was a keen fisherman ever since he was a child. He would take out his makeshift fishing rod, and fish by the rivers, the rocks, the seaside and even the storm-drains. He had always dreamt of fishing out at sea with his own boat. He would imagine the traps he would set and the fishing rods and lines he would need and more importantly, the different kinds of exotic fishes he would catch.

Once he was old enough to work, he started saving up for a fishing boat. Eventually, he set up a business which brought him a steady income and he was able to save up enough for a brand new fishing boat. The long fiberglass boat had fast beautiful engines, and he was keen to bring it out to sea. He brought his father who knew a thing or two about motorboats. Back then, no one needed (or cared about getting) a class 9 boat operator's license. You could just get a boat and put it to sea at your own risk.

They got the boat and its trailer to the Jerudong jetty on an early Saturday morning, just after dawn. The moment the boat started to float in the small cove, Ali jumped in exuberance.

The twin Yamaha boat engines chugged and then revved, pushing the boat faster and faster across the small waves and out onto the open sea. Ali's father reminded Ali to always keep his eye on land. They did not really understand navigation, but they knew if the weather turned, they would immediately set for land. They did not understand how dangerous it was not to know about navigation and GPS (global positional system).

Their boat was now some distance away from the shore. Everything on shore seemed very small. Ali could see some of the other small fishing boats far from them. He figured if they were in trouble, they could always head towards them or signal them with a mirror somehow or just shout really loudly.

They set their fishing rods whilst his father tried dropping down some makeshift crab and fish traps. His father was used to fishing in the river and not the sea.

Within a few minutes, both Ali and his father noticed their fishing lines were tugging. His father was the first to engage in the slow tug-of-war-tease with the fish. The idea was to wear the fish down and when the fish was finally tired and worn out, you could reel in the fish.

Ali checked on his line. His line was strange. Every time he was about to reel in the line a bit, the tugging had stopped. The tugging on his line was very rhythmic - as though it was like Morse code.

"That would be crazy," Ali thought.

He decided he should reel in his fishing line completely and inspect the hook, in case it was damaged or had caught on to something.

From where the fishing line had entered the water several meters away from the boat, he could see what looked like floating seagrass. He squinted hard, doing his best to focus in the reflection of the water. Ali could see a pair of green eyes. He could make out half of a very fair face, with beautiful green eyes and golden long hair. He gasped in disbelief. He shook his head hard and looked again. This time, he could see her smile. She was looking at him. He rubbed his eyes for a while and looked at the same spot. This time she winked at him. He could no longer doubt that he was looking at the head of a very pretty lady with golden hair in the sea.

Logic and fear overcame him. He cut his line with his pocket knife and shouted at his dad that they had to change position; they had to bring the boat much closer to shore. His father protested, "What about the traps?"

Ignoring his father, he started the boat engines, hands trembling as he prayed the engines would work. He could imagine a thousand bad scenarios. Luckily, the engines responded and he directed the boat towards the shore.

In his mind, Ali wondered what had happened. He thought it must have been a hallucination. He had never experienced a hallucination but there was no way that could have been human.

Ali cut off the engine when they reached a midway point from the shore and their original spot. The other fishing boats were closer but yet far away. His father was annoyed, but decided to trust his son's instincts.

His father set out his fishing line again, whilst Ali decided to have a cigarette first. He took his fishing rod and tied a new fishing lure and hook. He casted the line far away from the boat and watched it sink into the sea. In his mind, he was wondering why of all people, he was the one to have seen whatever 'she' was. He felt nauseous and retched. His father was too busy tending to his own fishing gear. He didn't want to tell his father what he had seen. He knew it was taboo to do so out at sea.

When Ali had finished his cigarette, he was able to brush off the whole incident. He looked at his line - nothing was biting for now. He decided he should scoop out some water from inside the boat. As he poured out the water back into the sea, he could see the same set of translucent green eyes staring back at him. She was closer to him, peering from next to the boat.

This time he could see her bare shoulders and noticed that her face and the rest of her skin was very fair and slightly pink. He was mesmerised by her beauty and her golden wet hair. She was smiling at him, and he could see her sharp but small canines. He could sense that her seemingly sweet smile hid evil intentions. A part of him wanted to reach his hand out and caress her, whilst the other part of him wanted to scream in terror and run away. Ali cautiously stepped away from the edge of the boat. He sat stumped and put his hands onto his face.

'I must be going crazy,' he thought.

And then it happened; he could hear a sound from the bow. He looked forward and saw the woman had climbed aboard. Half of her body had clambered on to the bow of the fishing boat. Dripping wet, she lied flat and used her hands to move the rest of her body into the boat. He could not see the lower half of her body.

Ali screamed and ran towards her, pushing her body off the boat. His father did not seem to care about the commotion. Ali pushed her at her shoulders, which was covered with translucent slippery slime. She was still smiling at him, as she clawed onto his forearms. Wedging himself against the boat, he pulled his arms away from her, as her sharp fingernails scratched down both his arms. He yelled in agony and then jumped hastily towards the stern and restarted the engines.

His father was baffled, asking Ali what was happening. Ali did not care. He needed to start the engines and get the hell out of there. The engine refused to start. He pushed the start button again, and frantically played with the throttle but the engine did not respond. Pain gripped his wounded forearms, which he tried to ignore, as his father and him were in imminent danger.

Shouting 'God was Great', Ali literally kicked the dead engines with his feet. He pushed the red start button and the engine came alive. He pushed the throttle all the way up to full speed. His father fell on to the float, cursing furiously, as they sped away leaving their fishing gear behind.

The boat rocked hard as it rode above the crests of the waves and crashed on each trough. His father was yelling for Ali to stop as he struggled to get back on to his feet.

Ali did not look back, he did not reduce the speed until they were near the Jerudong Beach cove.

He did not say a single word to his father, who was demanding an explanation for their spoilt fishing trip. Even after they got the boat back on to the trailer and the boat back home into their garage, Ali did not say a single word.

It was only after a few days that Ali was able to tell his father what had happened. Ali's father told him it was the right thing to do. Ali's father concluded that if he had been lured or if she had gotten onboard, both of them would surely be dead.

****

When Bob heard this story for the first time, he thought this was a funny mermaid story. It was simply difficult to believe. As a matter of fact, when I heard from Bob the first time, I laughed hard and told him there was no way this story could have been true. It sounded like a mermaid encounter and that can't be true.

However, every time Bob met his friend, the story was always the same, the details were always consistent. He told me he thought it was a Jinn that dwelled in the sea.

Bob also shared with me a conversation he had overheard between two sea captains at a local cafe. One of them was a local captain whilst the other was a Caucasian (European) who had recently arrived in Brunei and was about to start work.

"Anything interesting about the sea around Brunei?" asked the European officer.

"Mermaids!" replied the local captain.

The European sea captain laughed hard and then stopped when he realised the local captain was being very serious.

The Twins

Original story by Mr. M.

It is very strange that once I had moved out of that haunted apartment, more information about the strange happenings at that apartment become known to me. From the moment I had moved out, new friends and acquaintances would readily share their experiences and stories at the haunted apartment. I wish I had known this information before moving in there. I definitely would have thought twice or thrice before moving in.

Anyway, back to the story, after I had moved out and found a new place, I started finding out more about my previous flat. I found out that the area had a history of paranormal disturbances.

One of my friends used to live with her family on the first floor. She has two daughters who are identical twins. She told me they were both 'sensitive', they could see 'other worldly beings.' Some people say it meant they were gifted, but it hardly seemed like a 'gift'. It was more like a curse. The girls would cry a lot and out of the blue, would become quite hysterical. As a mother, she often wondered sadly, what the future would hold for her daughters and her family, especially when the twins refused to sleep in their own rooms, let alone stay by themselves in the apartment.

Even their nanny had frequently felt spooked out, once describing that it was like being constantly aware that someone was watching them. Their nanny did not work for them long after that.

According to my friend, her daughters would see mysterious shadows lurking near them. This would usually happen when they were playing on their own and no one else was there. At first, they tried to ignore it and carry on. However, when they least expected it, the dark shadows would move on their own and rush towards them, trying its best to grab the two girls.

In the beginning, the shadows were taunting the girls, making them run out of the room quickly. Then it became worse, the shadows would grow and move on to the ceiling. It would then randomly branch out to all four corners of the room, like the roots of an evil tree. The girls would always rush out of the room in time before the whole room was engulfed in complete darkness. Whatever it was, the girls were convinced that it was after their souls. They would scream hysterically whilst trying to explain to their parents.

My friend eventually sought the help of a local 'spiritual' expert to cleanse the area of the spirit. The family had also set up candles outside their door to ward off the spirit or spirits. For several days, all seemed peaceful. Whatever it was, had seemingly gone.

One day, the girls decided to play downstairs at the playground of the apartment. The mother made sure the nanny went with them. The playground was basically a well-trimmed grass area, in the middle of which stood a solitary dead hollow tree.

Suddenly, both girls froze, fell on to the green grass and started shaking violently! Their nanny instinctively started praying and tried to rouse the children. Failing that, the nanny frantically screamed for their mom. Her voice could be heard from the ground floor, all the way to the first floor. My friend ran down immediately and joined the nanny in prayer.

After what seemed like hours when it was only a few minutes, the two girls stopped their violent seizures. Their mom and the nanny carried them into the flat and administered 'smelling salts'.

When the girls regained consciousness, the twins immediately screamed again which startled the two adults. When things had subsided and everyone had calmed down, the girls mentioned they had seen a ghostly lady coming out from inside the tree and it was trying to take them into the tree.

After meeting with a few spiritual healers, they found out that that tree, which was very visible from their window, was apparently the home of a spirit lady who frequently appeared to the children.

After that incident, the family decided to move out and leave the place.

The Drive

Low, a Chinese man in his mid-forties commuted frequently between Kota Kinabalu (KK) and Limbang. He was a farmer who would bring vegetables and farm goods from his small farm to the market and restaurants in Kota Kinabalu.

His wife had died a few years ago, leaving him with his only son. His mother lived with him. His mother had once dreamt that her son would die horribly in a car crash, which got her to constantly worry about Low's frequent trips. She had also been regularly giving donations to the local Buddhist monk. His mother would also give away food and sometimes money to the orphanages and local schools. Low would get quite irate with his mother, especially since Low was not doing too well in his farming business. His mother would tell him to stop being a miser. She said she was not happy that he was always talking about money, whilst she had to constantly remind him that she raised him to be a generous kind man.

One day, after a big fight, his mother felt unwell and had to be hospitalised. The doctors had told Low that she had stroke. She thought she could save some money for her son and not buy her medication for her hypertension. Low broke down, he wished he had not bickered about trying to save money, and now his mother was very unwell.

Low wanted to remain next to his bedridden mother but he could not stay long in the hospital as he still had to work. He suddenly wished he had hired delivery drivers. He reasoned he had not done so as he did not trust anyone else to deliver his produce.

Now, he had another problem. There was no one to take care of his 5-year-old son. He did not like the idea of leaving his son with anyone else but his mother. Low decided to bring his son with him. It would be a good opportunity to spend time together, let him watch what his father does for a living. He wondered that perhaps his son would take over his farm when he grows up. Low didn't want to admit it, but he was feeling extremely sad and he couldn't bear the thought of driving alone to KK and Limbang.

On their way there, they made a stop at Lawas town. They had their late breakfast and toilet break at a local restaurant. It was his regular restaurant and everyone knew Low. The restaurant owner and waiters commented on how Low's son was a spitting image of him, but much younger and more handsome!

They noticed an elderly man sitting quietly on the roadside curb. His clothes were dirty and were in tatters. Low's son approached the old man. Low asked the waiters who the elderly man was, but they seemed to ignore him.

Low approached the elderly man himself. He noticed the man was unkempt and he had long disheveled hair. He also reeked of urine. A part of Low wanted to kick the man away from his son, but he remembered his mother's words. He recalled the number of times his mother reminded him to be charitable and less judgmental.

Low asked the man if he was hungry and the man nodded. Low got some bananas from his small truck. He also got out a couple of aubergines - which were his mother's favourites. The man smiled, unintentionally revealing his crooked and rotting teeth. Low did his best not to cringe. He got his son to buy takeaway food from the restaurant, which he then gave to the old man. He gave him some money too. The elderly man thanked the two of them and wished them all the best in their lives.

Low and his son got back into their truck and drove on. Low couldn't help from wondering if he did the right thing. He kept asking himself how much money he had 'lost'. He calculated how much he would lose in a year if he met the same old man every time he was at that restaurant. A part of him regretted giving away food and money to the old man. Of course, his mother's words echoed in his heart and mind. It was a spiral of sadness as the two thoughts clashed over and over again.

When Low reached Kota Kinabalu, he delivered the vegetables and farm produce to the markets and the restaurants. His last delivery was to a large popular restaurant, whom he had been doing business with for more than a decade. He was expecting to collect a large payment from them, which was really credit that they owed him. The owner insisted Low give him a large discount otherwise he would not get a single cent. Low had to bitterly concede.

He cried in the truck, he didn't care his son was watching. He was finding life difficult. He kept asking himself why was his life difficult. A million dark thoughts entered his thoughts - 'the call of the void' - but were repelled when his son hugged him.

"It's alright, Papa. I wish grandma was not unwell," his son did his best to fight his sobs in between his words.

Low wiped his tears, embraced his son and made up his mind to bring his son around KK. A father and son - little sightseeing trip. They had gone around to a beach and hung around the malls. Low bought his son new clothes which he wore immediately. They didn't notice how fast time had flown, and it was nearly nighttime. Low had to decide if he was going to spend some money and stay at a hotel or drive home through the night. Low thought the latter was better. In any case, if he was too tired, he could always park by the roadside and sleep in the truck. It was a good plan.

However, after driving past Sipitang, there was a sudden downpour. The wind howled loudly as it blew against the truck, pushing it slowly from its intended course. The tropical storm was in full force. Its raindrops were so large and continuous, it looked like a thick white curtain of continuous raging stream from the night sky. Low had to drive slowly, doing his best to keep his truck from veering off the road. He was tired but the adrenaline from the fear of being killed along with his son in an accident kept him wide awake. He remembered his mother's prophetic dream that he would be killed in a road accident.

A passing truck splashed water on his windscreen, turning his vision to a blurred wish wash of orange and dark colours. Low heard a loud screech and the sound of cars in front of him crashing. Low lost control of his small truck as it hydroplaned on the road, veering on its own course. Low braked hard but the truck did not respond. Low prepared for the worst, he placed his arm across his son's chest in a futile attempt to stop the inevitable. His mother's prophecy was becoming a reality!

Low had kept his eyes closed, waiting for the impact. As the seconds slowed to a standstill, Low opened his eyes and saw the bright light outside his truck. He wondered if this was heaven. He used the windscreen wiper to clear the wet windscreen.

Low could not understand what he was seeing. The truck was on an unpaved dirt road, and it was daytime. The sun was shining brightly in the sky. On both sides of the road, he could see rice paddy fields. Low wondered if somehow, he had gone off the road and got onto this road and fell asleep. That was not possible, he thought.

Not knowing what to make of it, he decided to drive on and see what was at the end of the road. Low's son commented on the birds flying in the sky. Low looked up and saw the birds were huge. He thought they were as large as a small plane. They also looked like birds of prey. The birds were high up in the sky. Low started to chant a prayer, begging for protection.

As he drove on, he saw people in the waterlogged paddy fields. They were all dressed in black and even had black conical farmers' hats. Low stopped the truck and got out. He wanted to ask for help from the farmers but was overwhelmed by an uneasiness. His legs trembled in fear. He noticed that none of them were looking at him. In actual fact, Low could not see any of their faces. Low told his son not to point at the 'farmers'. Instinctually, he knew they were not normal people and wherever they were, it was not anywhere near Sipitang, or home for that matter. Low jumped back into his truck and drove on faster.

The road did not seem to have an end. The faster he drove on it, the further the road seemed. Low thought he saw something in the distance. There was a darkness up ahead. He tried to stop the truck but the truck moved on its own. Neither the steering wheel nor the brakes responded. Low was too scared to jump out of his truck.

As the road disappeared, the truck entered a dark black hole. Low's son started waving, "It's Po Po! Bye Po Po!" Low scrambled to his son's seat and peered out to see but he could not see his mother.

The truck was completely immersed in the black void. It stopped moving, and the engine cut out on its own. Low sensed impending doom. He covered his son with his body. He must protect him to the end. Low cried loudly and his son cried with him.

Trembling in fear, the truck began to vibrate and shake, tapping and drumming all over. His eyes shut tight, and yet he could see flashes of white light followed by a loud bang, a crash that sounded all too familiar. He opened his eyes, and looked through the windscreen.

Low could see a familiar house up ahead. It was his house. The lights have been left on, and he could see the rain pouring down on its corrugated steel roofing. He scanned around to confirm he was near his house compound. Low had a hard time believing it, he opened the door a bit and put out his hand. His hand became wet and cold. He knew this was home. He started the truck and slowly drove into his garage.

When Low settled home, he got a call from the hospital, to say his mother had just died. Low slumped in his chair and fell asleep. When he woke up, he knew he had to make funeral arrangements for his mother.

A few days later, he found out there was a terrible accident that involved a number of trucks and cars near Sipitang. There were many fatalities; it was deemed the worst accident for that year. Low often wondered what had actually happened. He wondered how the truck got from Sipitang area to his house. To this day, he has no answers.

After that incident, Low often gave alms and donations to people who were in need. Over the next few years, his farming business thrived and he hired drivers to deliver his farm produce.

The Crossing

I had met a middle-aged nurse who was working at a clinic in Kuala Belait town. She had decided to share her story with me but had wished to remain anonymous.

It was back in the 1990s when she was still in her late 20s. Joanna (not her real name) was a bubbly single nurse who loved hanging around with her three girlfriends, who were also working in the same ward. When they were not working the same night shifts, they would usually go out at night and only return home when it was very late. Everybody knew everyone in Belait and it was a very safe place. This would be their typical female YUPPIE (young urban professional) night. She and her friends would chill out at the local cafes, watch the men and the boys approach them with their terrible 'pick-up lines', and turn their lover-boy hopes and dreams into ashes and dust. Life was too young and too fun to be in a serious relationship.

Sometimes, they had to leave early. One big signal for them to head home was if it started to rain. Joanna and her friends were not superstitious. They were practical. Nobody should be driving when it rains heavily.

One fateful night, the rain that had started as a bare drizzle quickly became a full-on monsoon downpour. The wind howled vengefully at their car as they drove slowly on Maulana Road. This was the main road from Kuala Belait to Seria, where they all lived. The rain hammered relentlessly on to their small car, drowning out their loud music. Joanna decided to turn off the car stereo so that her friend could concentrate on driving. The visibility was very poor. The orange sodium lights were barely visible, but at least they knew they were on the correct path. They could see the cars in front of them, crawling slowly.

As they were nearing the Istana or palace, the traffic had stopped to a complete standstill. Joanna could see in front of them were about six cars that had stopped. Joanna wondered if there was an accident up ahead. She thought about the inexperienced drivers who had ended up in the local hospital (or worse) because they misjudged the rain and drove too fast. It was at that moment, in front of the first car in the traffic jam, that she saw 'it'.

She gasped. She heard her friend Ayu, gasped too. Joanna didn't want to believe it. She tried to convince herself it was an illusion of the mind, an optical illusion due to the poor visibility and heavy rain.

She held her breath as she asked herself what exactly had she seen. Joanna turned to Ayu, and tried to muster courage, to ask Ayu if she had seen 'it'. Before she could utter a single word, the car heaved to the left. The wind blew even harder. Joanna wondered if the wind could have really pushed the car that way.

By instinct, Ayu looked to her right window and then quickly closed her eyes, slumping her head towards the steering wheel. She was muttering something and crying. Her friends in the back seat let out a short cry when they saw what was on the side of the car.

Joanna could see through the window, a black shape, which she thought was the lower end of a giant black leg. There was another short heave and she could see the dark object disappear from the right side of the car, moving over the car and appearing on the left side.

Her friends in the back seats ducked in prone position, praying for their lives. The dark leg moved away from the car and headed towards the beach and the sea. As it 'walked' away from the car, she could see its true shape, a black humanoid giant, which was much taller than the streetlights.

None of the cars moved for at least 15 minutes, as the downpour continued, casting white shadowy glimmers on to the line of cars. When the rain began to subside, more cars turned up and started sounding their horns, and all of the cars started moving.

Their drive back home was a quiet and solemn affair. Not a single word, as they did their best to muffle their sobs.

When Joanna got home, she got to her bed quickly. She left a light on as she stared onto the ceiling. She knew there was no way she could sleep that night. She kept on recalling what she saw in front of the line of cars and then the dark mysterious giant that had walked over their car and then headed its way to the beach.

The next day at work, Joanna and her friends pretended to be their usual jovial self, but it was obvious last night's incident hung in the air like a dark cloud. It was only during lunchtime, Ayu blurted out she had to send the car for a car wash, as she had peed herself and onto the car seat from last night's incident.

Usually, a confession like that would have sent the ladies into raucous laughter. Instead, the other girls hugged Ayu in a warm consoling embrace. Tears streamed down their faces as they all shared how scared they were. They realised what they saw must have been an 'Orang Tinggi' spirit. None of them had ever seen one, let alone had such a supernatural encounter.

Ayu mentioned that she first saw the dark figure crossing the road, which was probably the reason why the other cars had stopped. Joanna then told everyone that whilst Ayu was looking away, she saw other shadow giants crossing the road too. She was sure she had seen four or five of the Orang Tinggi demons. One of them stopped and stared into their car. It was strange that immediately after that, one had 'walked over' their car.

Since that incident, the girls would go back earlier from their local cafes and would hang out at each other's homes. This would usually turn into a sleepover, which was far better than driving back home in the middle of the night.

The Room

This story was contributed by Khadijah Marali who is a 13-year-old student at SMPAPHM secondary school. She is a horror movie fan, who would always end up shouting at the television screen when one of the characters decides to go towards the source of the disturbance.

In 2015, she had an encounter in Luagan Dudok village in Tutong whilst visiting her grandmother and her cousins.

***

I woke up feeling queasy. My eyes wandered towards the clock; 12:00 pm. I would always get a headache whenever I oversleep. I grumbled in frustration as I rolled out of bed and made my way to the bathroom. I noticed my sister was not too cheerful too as she crawled out of bed.

After showering, I made my way to the kitchen where brunch was waiting. I was about to play with my iPad, when my mother reminded me of the house rule i.e. no gadgets when eating.

The three of us had a small chat about our upcoming trip to Grandmother's house. We were not just visiting Grandmother but we were also meeting up with my cousins. After brunch, I ran to my bedroom and prepared the things for the trip. There was one thing that was very important to me: my bulky orange cased iPad mini. I hugged it dearly before placing it in my bag.

We rushed into the car, as we did our best to evade the blinding sunlight and sweltering tropical heat. The air conditioner of the car gave us relief as a reward for our mad dash. It is strange that our lives in equatorial Brunei would involve running from one air-conditioned room to another.

Whilst in the car and listening to music, my thoughts drifted to thoughts of Tutong. I pondered upon the simple life in Tutong and then I thought about my grandmother and her house. My grandmother's house was really old, it was ancient to be exact. My mom and her five siblings grew up, shared their rooms; and more importantly, shared their memories together inside that house.

Suddenly, my mind thought about the paranormal stuff that happened in that house. I had overheard 'encounters' other family members had. Since my grandmother's house was near the forest, I guess you could say there were a lot of 'people' in the house. That was one of the reasons why the elders, especially my grandmother, would forbid us from playing outside after sunset. She reasoned that we may see 'things'.

My grandmother is the type of person who always believes in superstitions and the untrue information on the internet. Some of her superstitions or 'pantangs' include not having naps between 3pm to 5pm (because according to her, you would have bad dreams that evening). She also believes that we should never ever whistle (because she believes you would be calling 'it'). There were many others and to me, none of them made sense. It was just superstition.

I managed to sleep for half an hour in the car. When we finally arrived at Grandmother's house, I grabbed my things and stepped out onto the familiar rocky pavement leading to her house.

My grandmother was standing near the door. I greeted her eagerly with a tight embrace. I had noticed the house seemed empty. My uncle and his wife had gone out. I checked the living room, then my grandmother's room and the old storeroom. I quickly ran back to the main room because an eerie feeling of a 'presence' overwhelmed me.

There was no one there and yet I could not fight the feeling. 'Scaredy cat,' I blamed myself. My gaze strayed towards the stairway. There was this feeling of something calling me to that place. I went up the stairway as my fingers ran along the rough wooden hand rail. When I went upstairs, I found nothing and yet there was that unexplained feeling that I was not alone.

My eyes can't help to be drawn to this upstairs room. The room used to be late grandfather's room. We had only discovered it several weeks ago as it was essentially a hidden storeroom. We had cleaned and tidied it. My cousins and I had made the decision that this would be the place where we would hang out. Although the room could use renovations, it was as ready as it was. I went back downstairs and went to my cousin's room.

"Hadi it's me!" I said.

"Come on in!" Hadi replied, I could hear the smile in his voice.

"Hey Cuz, what's up! Long time no see, I've missed you!" I said, fist bumping him. "Me too!" he replied. We switched on our iPads and played whilst the sound of our laughter and loud conversations filled the room. Our gaming was interrupted by a very loud roar of laughter. We could hear familiar shrill voices outside. Hadi and I ran to greet our newly-arrived cousins.

We raced to our upstairs room, laughing and teasing the ones who got left behind. Hadi ended up winning the race whilst I got second place. He switched on the lights as the others sat down on the carpet.

I could not help from noticing that it was much cleaner than usual. The only annoying thing was that there was a glass table blocking the sofa, which made the room more cramped than usual.

We played multiplayer games on our iPads again. At around 3pm, my cousins, Mariam, Iman dan Diwi barged into the room. It felt like forever waiting for them. My other two 'emotionless' cousins; Amin and Maya quietly slid through the rowdy bunch and whispered their greetings with a monotonous whisper. Finally, all of us were here.

However, the room was silent as all of us were playing on our gadgets- which by right was a fine display of anti-social behaviour.

Out of the blue, my sister Nora had an idea, "How about we play 'Carah' and 'Carah Bertapuk'?" She would always be the one to come up with these strange games.

All of us immediately dropped our iPads and phones, as if we forgot technology existed. "YAYY!" we screamed, ecstatically. We had our own version of hide-and-seek and tag.

"Switch off the lights! It'll be much more fun!" said Hadi. We all agreed.

The best way to decide who was going to be 'it' was a trial of rock, paper and scissors. Diwi was it and this was the most odd, creepy and perfect person to fit the role of the 'seeker'. She doesn't walk to find someone. Instead, she would crawl in an awkward manner whilst intentionally grunting!

Our screaming, laughter and giggles could be heard outside the room. We played the game for two rounds. It was pretty exhausting but it was fun. We decided the third round would be the last.

"Diwi, close your eyes and spin three times!" my sister instructed. Diwi did so as we scrambled to our hiding spots. I found a hiding spot near the door in the corner of the room with my cousin Alliya. Across from us I could see my sister and Hadi trying their best to stifle their laughter. Amin sat near the corner of the room. There was nothing to hide behind so he held a pillow in front of his face.

'Why is he holding a pillow as a weapon?' I snickered.

Luck was not on his side as Diwi came closer to Amin. Her eyes were shut tight as per game rules as she searched with her hands anything that was in front of her. Amin sat quietly, his own eyes closed as Diwi reached out to Amin. Amin kept the pillow in front of him.

"... Oh it's just the pillow," Diwi muttered and shrugged, unbothered. Amin was so happy that he had not been caught yet. We all tried not to laugh. Suddenly, we heard Mariam scream out. Diwi had captured a person and now the game was over.

In the midst of all the laughter, I heard Hadi and Adam whispering softly but I did not give it much thought.

We told Diwi about Amin and the pillow incident- she laughed uncontrollably. We decided to have a break and went downstairs. After having some refreshments. I plopped down on the floor, cooling off under the ceiling fan. I could see Adam was walking in circles and he was fidgeting nervously.

"Adam, are you okay?" I asked.

"Ah.." He trailed off, before saying, "Actually- no. Where were you hiding Ijah?" he suddenly asked.

"Oh um, near the door at the corner of the room. Why?" I replied. I thought it was weird to ask since I was sure he should have seen where I was hiding. After all, the room wasn't that big.

Adam was silent at first. Slowly, he spoke out, "Oh.. I- um, saw 'you' under the table. I called you out. Hadi had looked but he said there was no one there."

"When I looked again under the table, it wasn't there anymore," he said frowning, "It was a weird and creepy version of 'you', it had eyes that looked like yours but it was bigger... twice as big..."

My cousin shuddered as the hairs on my arms rose on their own.

"You- no, 'It' had this huge smile across its face when I called you out.. Its lips were stretched out and was... unnatural," he muttered.

"Oh- wow. I don't know how to process this," I mumbled, shocked.

Adam nodded, "Me too... I am lucky that 'you' didn't harm me," he said. He turned to me with a serious glint in his eyes, out of character than his usual goofy self, "What did you think it was?"

"Adam, I'm not sure," was all I could muster the courage to say.

The Keeper

I had known Rosnah, a middle-aged lady, for at least 10 years before I had left the government service. I loved seeing her as she seemed to have the latest social news or gossip in Tutong. I would tell my fellow doctor colleagues that I was simply collecting 'societal intelligence' which may or may not affect my clinical decisions! Surprisingly her insights (and gossips) were pretty accurate. Sometimes I wish I had done a study about 'social news networks.' Before I had left, she had shared with me a story that I am sure was not unique. There were others who were in similar situations.

Rosnah lived in a small village in Tutong. She shared her house with her elderly parents, her siblings, all their children and of course two maids. It was typical to have many family members living under one roof. There were many benefits of living in extended households. However, Rosnah's brother, Rahim, decided he was going to build his own house next to the main house. He was already a senior government officer and his wife, who was not from Tutong, was finding it a bit suffocating to not have her own privacy. Rahim and his wife had three children and were planning to have more. The family understood and consented for Rahim to build his own house. Rahim's house was a double story house, complete with a Mediterranean design, which was not appropriate for a tropical country, but it was their house and their choice of style.

A year after Rahim had moved into the new house, Rahim's application to undertake his Master's degree in the United Kingdom was approved. It meant that his wife and his three children went along with him, and they would stay with him for the next 12 months or so. Their house was; of course, left locked and vacant. It was accepted that Rahim's wife did not like any of her in-laws to rifle through their belongings. It was not a Tutong thing to do but for the sake of family peace, everyone accepted that was the way things were.

Whilst Rahim and his family were away, Rosnah started to notice strange things. For starts, both maids were always extremely reluctant to perform any tasks outside the house after dusk. It was getting annoying when spoilt vegetables and fruits were still in the kitchen and not in the garbage bins outside. Each maid was always trying to get the other to do the job. Even in the midst of a string of house burglaries in the house, both maids were not willing to go out at night to lock the front gate. This happened even when it was suggested that the both of them go out together. Every time Rosnah asked, both maids kept quiet.

One day, just after dawn, Rosnah's mother went to the kitchen. The night before, there was a large family function and there were some leftover dishes to be washed. She didn't want the maids to sleep late, so she said she would wash some of the dishes in the morning. The large kitchen faced their backyard, which had a few mango and coconut trees, and then further away was the jungle. She was reminiscing the conversation she had with her sister when she glimpsed a black streak going slowly across the backyard. She squinted and saw that the long black streak was connected to a head with a pale face, and attached to a female body in a white dress.

'It' was floating strangely in mid-air. Its hair was so long that it seemed to stretch from one end of the backyard to the other. Rosnah's mother dropped the plate she was washing. She did not breathe for fear the apparition would notice her. Rosnah's mother gazed wildly as she watched the floating lady head towards the neighbouring house i.e. Rahim's house. It floated through the wall of the house and disappeared, but not before staring intently at Rosnah's mother. She held her chest tight and struggled to breathe. She thought she was going to die on the spot. Within a few minutes, Rosnah's mother's breathing had gotten back to normal.

Rosnah's mother was thoroughly shaken and felt unwell after that day. After a few days, she confided to Rosnah about what she had seen. She told Rosnah not to tell anyone else. This was poor judgement on her mother's part.

Of course, as you can guess, Rosnah could not keep it as a secret. In less than a few hours, the whole family had known, including Rosnah's father - who in spite of his old age, was still very temperamental. The family wanted to know why 'it' entered Rahim's house. Everyone suspected there was something supernatural inside Rahim's house.

The family resisted all temptations to call Rahim and talk about these matters over the phone. The good news was that Rahim had to come back to Brunei for a new job posting interview in the next few weeks.

Over the next few weeks, there were no more sightings, but now that everyone was aware, all observations were noted and shared. Everything that had previously been dismissed as wild imagination, had formed its own conclusion.

For example, the children had always felt as though someone was watching them every time they played in the compound of Rahim's house. Sometimes, they would hear a faint cackling sound. Worst of all, all the stories that the pre-teen children told about the lady in white playing hide and seek suddenly made sense!

None of the adults believed them back then, but now they did. By now, the maids confessed to all their sightings. They had been chased by the 'floating lady in white' as they tried to close the front gate or to throw rubbish at night. At times, they would be woken up in the middle of the night by knocking on their window and a floating silhouette, which they assumed had to be the ghost with the very long hair.

The family decided it was best not to invite any spiritual masters until Rahim came back. It was his house after all. More importantly, their village was a tight-knit community and they didn't want the family to be picked by the usual rumour mill.

Soon enough, Rahim, his wife and his children came back to Brunei and were staying in their house for the next ten days. They were to fly back to the UK after that. This was more than enough time to confront them.

Rosnah's parents had asked them to attend the family dinner. It was just going to be the parents and the siblings. All the grandchildren were to dine in a separate room.

Rosnah's father did not hold back. He revealed to Rahim the apparitions they had seen and how it had always ended up entering Rahim's house. Rahim's father wondered loudly if his eldest son was dumb enough to be a deviant by choosing to keep or 'pelihara' a supernatural entity in their house.
It was the most uncomfortable family dinner ever. Rosnah's father was literally yelling at his son. Fortunately, Rahim knew his father well and apologised to the family. He confessed that his wife

and himself thought they needed to make sure their house did not get burgled especially whilst they were away for a long time. They had a 'penjaga' or a keeper spirit that would fend away thieves and undesirables.

It was at this moment, Rosnah's father stood up and told the other siblings to leave. Rahim and his wife were to stay. It was a very private harsh scolding, that left both middle-aged adults sobbing and constantly begging for forgiveness for their lack of poor judgement.

Rosnah; who could not help herself from eavesdropping, remembered her father kept going on and on about doing the right thing and never to take shortcuts in life. Entrusting or keeping spirits of any kind was not within their religious beliefs. If a house was to be burgled then that is fate. Rosnah's father kept on and on about repenting. By the time Rosnah's father was done, it was nearly 1am - he had been shouting, scolding and ranting for several hours.

Rahim had the spiritual entity removed and there were no further sightings. Sure enough, as soon as Rahim and his family left for the UK, his house was burgled in broad daylight! Of course, that had been fated.

When Rahim came back home and settled, he invested in a secure CCTV and participated in neighbourhood watch (patrols) and eventually cared less about his privacy and frequently let his siblings and their children freely hangout at his house.

Rosnah's father kept reminding Rahim that love was about sharing, that is their way.

Skylight

This story was contributed by Adrina Hj Mohd Agus Din, a passionate English teacher from Rimba 2 Secondary School.

It was almost 'Maghrib' as I ushered my 2 children inside the house for bath time. They had been riding their bicycles for over an hour and I was optimistic they would both be tired enough for an early bedtime. Aden was three whilst Ayesha was one, and both were always a handful.

My maid carried Ayesha in and I took Aden to the driveway to hose down the bicycles. He loved playing with water. However this time, Aden started crying as we got closer to the garden hose. He refused to walk and fell heavily into my arms. I did not think much of it. I thought he was just tired so I left the bicycles and carried him into the house.

Inside, the house was a flurry of activity. The bath tub was filled with bubbles and the kids were happy. Dinner was always a messy affair with lumps of food ending up on the floor rather than the children's mouths. My home was blessed with so much laughter.

It was almost bedtime now. Aden and I were reading on the sofa while my husband Pete and Ayesha were playing with blocks on the carpet. As Aden sang, he started laughing and pointed to the window behind us.

"Mama, look, that man has no face."

"What man, love?" I thought he was describing the picture in his book.

Aden jumped off the sofa and ran to the window, pulling the curtains aside to reveal our driveway, "That man, Mama. Hello No-face!"

I panicked and closed the curtains quickly. I knew immediately what he was talking about. There was no way I was going to peek through the windows. Pete looked at me in disbelief.

"Time for bed!" I screamed a little too loudly and grabbed the kids' arms to go upstairs. Pete whispered that he was going to walk around outside our garden and to lock the gate. Pete opened the front door and the eerie sweet scent of flowers flooded our living room. I begged him not to go outside and we took the kids to bed.

Pete and I tried hard not to show the kids how spooked we were. As the kids were finally safe in bed, I recited a few prayers and hoped we would be protected that night.

In the middle of the night, Aden crawled into our bed. For some reason, he was laughing. Glancing at the alarm clock, I saw that it was 3am. I thought Aden had simply wanted to sleep with us, which was usual for him. I pulled the duvet cover expecting him to slip in. Instead, he pointed to the window above my bed.

"No-face!" he giggled and tried to climb over me, arms stretched out to the window.

Oh no, here we go again.

"He is so tall! Why doesn't he have a face Mama?" Aden was looking intently at the window now, his gaze unwavering.

"He wants me to go outside. He said he had fun today. Can I go play with him, Mama?"

I woke Pete up and told him quickly what had happened. I hugged Aden and wouldn't let him go. We also noticed our house-cats which would usually sleep in the room were screeching and hissing. All five cats were staring at the skylight.

Pete and I could not see anything but we could sense there was something ominous there.

"What else do you see Aden?"

"There's lots of them, Mama. There is also a girl with long hair. She's flying."

At that moment, I felt really angry. How dare they disturb my little boy! I wanted to fight and scream. I wanted to shout out as many rude words as I could to those spirits.

Instead, I pretended to be calm. I said, " Aden, please tell them it's too late for you to play. You need to go to sleep."

I picked up Aden off the bed and put him onto his bed, carefully placing him as far away from the windows as possible. As I tucked him up, we heard it. The sharpest shrillest scream right outside the window Aden was staring at. The hairs on my neck straighten up, as a cold chill went down my spine.

Pete decided to take charge. He was not having any more of this, so he pulled the curtains open. Expecting the faces of death, but instead we saw nothing. I closed Aden's eyes with my hands and prayed. I recited every verse I could think of, whilst praying hard for protection.

Pete looked out the window. He placed his hands on the glass and pleaded,

"Please, leave him and Ayesha alone. They mean everything to us. Please don't hurt them."

We switched the lights on and I kept praying. At 5am, I could sense we were no longer in danger. We never heard from 'No-face' again.

The Shadow

This story was contributed and written by Nuuraaisyah Arman, a 13-year-old student at SMPAPHM secondary school . She loves to write and does artwork.

Here's a story of my encounter.

Rumors had it that the school was haunted. The school which I would not name was somewhere in Batu Satu in Bandar Seri Begawan. I used to study there.

It was the year 2016. My friends and I were on our way to the back of the school. That place was our hangout spot, where we would gaze upon a field of long green grass. There was also the old toilet and it was apparently a haunted place. We were either brave or did not care at all that we would plop down on the grass and did our own thing.

Everyone said it was haunted but none of my friends and I had ever had such an encounter. I guess it just meant that the place was our exclusive spot.

We did what children our age did. At least the ones with no electronic gadgets. We would look for insects and tumble into the long grass. We would roll ourselves onto the grass until we found patches of fungus. We were at least smart enough not to roll over the patch of fungus, though one of us would always try to push the other into it.

We also had our role-playing games. My favorite was the one where we would look for the well that was said to have a corpse at the bottom. It was an urban myth that became our role-play game story. Luckily, we never found that well. We would also play pretend as if we were in a kingdom or sometimes a cemetery. It was fun and that was our adventure time.

One day, as we sipped our sweet cordial drinks and munched on our candy bar snacks, we all agreed we were quite bored. For the past hour, we had been gossiping about stuff in school (like what we always did). We did our usual short silly games like the staring contest, truth or dare, wrestling and more. And yet we felt unsatisfied. We were so bored we even picked flowers and exchanged it with each other. My friend, Adibah, suggested a new (and yet old) game, "Hey, let's play hide and seek?" What a wonderful idea, we all thought.

After playing a few rounds of hide-and-seek, Haziyah became the seeker. She found me soon enough, in less than a minute. I thought I had found a good hiding spot. She figured that was where she would hide too. Anyway, I decided to help her out by looking for others. Soon enough, we found everyone else... except for Farah. We wondered out loudly where could Farah have hidden.

We split into three groups. Ainan and I, Adibah and Haziyah and Basirah with Zafirah. Ainan and I looked around every crook and cranny. We even went to look inside the staffroom. That was hard to explain to the teachers. Nevertheless, we had no luck in finding Farah. We felt a sense of urgency and started asking other students. But no one had seen Farah. When we walked back to our hangout spot, the others were not there yet.

"We haven't check that one place," Ainan told me, and I knew exactly where she meant. "The old toilet," Ainan told me. She had always wanted to explore that place and this was her opportunity. She dragged me there, although I protested initially.

The old toilet looked old and had dark green and black algae growing from every corner of the floor and walls. A damp smell hung in the air. We slowly walked pass each of the toilet stalls, slowly kicking each door open. No one was there. I wondered if we really should be doing this. Before I could convince Ainan to turn back, we noticed a shadow within the last remaining unchecked stalls. The feet and leg shadows looked like Farah. We were convinced it was Farah.

We were going to give her a good scare. We snuck near the toilet stall and kicked the door hard, whilst shouting "Boo!" To our surprise, there was no one there. Every bone in my body told me that we needed to get out of there. I grabbed Ainan's hand and rushed out as waves of chills ran down my spine. I could see fear in Ainan's eyes.

We got out of the toilet and did not look back and we did not stop until we got back to our safe hangout spot.

It was then that we heard the others. "Aaisyah! Ainan! We found Farah!"

Apparently, Farah had hid herself under the stairs and a cute cat came over; which of course, distracted her. Farah loves cats. Actually, we all do.

Ainan and I felt very unsettled. We did not talk about it until the next day at school. Our friends made funny jokes afterwards to lighten up the atmosphere. However, nothing changed for me. I would feel goosebumps all over every time I was near that toilet.

Recently, a friend told me that the junior students used that old toilet. They ignored the rumors. I guess they did not mind the 'shadow'.

The Car

Rashid would never forget the year 1986. It was the year the Space Shuttle Challenger (a spaceship for those who don't know) exploded. It was the year his youngest brother was born. It was the year his family had gotten that car.

His father, Tamin, had bought a car, which was an Audi 90. It was a second-hand car, sold at a bargain price. It was an exciting feeling to have a German car. You could say the family felt privileged. His father had bought a sports saloon car which was beige or brown in color. It had all the cool features and as a 10-year-old kid, he was very impressed. His 5-year-old brother was also impressed with the car. His mother, who was heavily pregnant then, was not happy with the newly acquired car. She was very suspicious that the car had been sold at such a cheap price by an owner who seemed keen to get rid of it. She asked Rashid's dad to have it inspected in case of any serious faults, but the mechanics said it was in perfect condition.

1986 was the start of Tamin's difficulties. He had built up debt in building a house and was constantly arguing with the construction company who was trying to swindle him. He worked in the construction industry, which gave him much insight. He didn't think the company would try to cheat him because of his background. Rashid's father, who was an inspirational man in his childhood, became an ill-tempered person to everyone including his own children. Rashid and his brother had to be careful about what they say and do. Otherwise, they would get a thorough scolding or worse.

Their joy with the new car was short-lived. Rashid's father began having minor car accidents. He would bump into streetlights and have parking accidents. He had a few accidents on the road with other cars too. The damage was cosmetic as it had always happened at slow speeds, but it stressed Rashid's parents further as it meant more expenses, which was not good whilst his father was already heavily in debt to the banks.

One evening, Rashid's father and mother had gone to a family function. Rashid and his brother stayed at home with the family maid. On the way back, his mother had suddenly screamed out loud. His father got shocked and brought the car to a screeching halt. Luckily there were no cars behind them. His mother was hysterical. She thought she saw a dark shadowy figure sitting behind them whilst she was looking at a mirror.

After that incident, Rashid's parents had placed prayer books inside the car. There could have been at least ten 'Surah Yassin' books inside.

The next day, the family had gone over to their cousin's house whilst Rashid's father was supervising the contractor; which he kept reminding, was not his job. That day, he uncovered a huge dangerous shortcut the construction company had made. He had had enough. He was livid. He could be heard shouting from a few houses away.

One of Rashid's uncles had given Tamin a Holy Quran. He had hoped Tamin would find his way back to God. Tamin had placed the Holy Quran book inside the boot of the car. He was not happy about being preached especially when he was already in a very foul mood.

By dusk, it was getting late and the sky had become dark grey overcast.

As the family got into the car, the downpour began. A full tropical rainstorm was in effect. They were heading to the Capital via 'Jalan Kebangsaan Lama' or the Kebangsaan Lama road. The orange sodium streetlights revealed the huge deep storm drains on both sides of the road had been completely filled up. Now rainwater overflowed and thinly covered the road.

The car drove on and as if it had a life of its own, veered to the left and into the storm drain! The water engulfed the windscreen, and Rashid's father told everyone to get out of the car immediately. He opened the door and cold rainwater rushed in.

Rashid was sitting next to the door and tried it. The door refused to budge. Their maid tried to open the door but she too could not open it. The car submerged in water, began to list to the right side. She tried to open the door again but felt a hand pulling her own hand away. She recited a prayer and the door finally opened. Rashid was the first one out. As he pushed himself towards the surface, he realized he did not know how to swim. He shouted for help. He saw a tree branch which seemed to lean over to rescue him. His mother grabbed him as she stood on the car. Everyone was out except for Rashid's brother. His father dived beneath the water to look for his brother.

Then Rashid realised that his brother was actually right beside him. When his father surfaced, they told him both his sons were there. That gave him much relief. Rashid looked around and had a hard time believing that they were all in the huge storm drain, standing on top of their fully submerged car. It was still raining heavily and a few passing motorists had stopped to see if they could help.

Eventually, the car listed back to its original position, which was possibly because the air pocket and the current had readjusted the car. The water level in the storm drain was still high and there was a fast current. They all had to stand huddled together on the roof of the car. They could see large broken tree branches floating past by, which was dangerous if any had struck them.

One of the passersby jumped into the water, swimming against the current. He reached for the family and rescued Rashid. After that, he swam back and rescued Rashid's brother. Rashid's father had to stay with his pregnant wife whilst another person rescued the family maid. When the water had subsided, Rashid's parents jumped and swam to the other side of the storm drain. They climbed over and walked on the edge of a fence, to safety.

When they got home, Rashid cried as he had lost his spectacles. Rashid's mother immediately embraced both her sons and tearfully told them that it was better to lose mere possessions than to lose their lives. She was very grateful that no one had lost their lives, especially her two sons.

The next day, Rashid's father had inspected their Audi car. He noticed the Holy Quran in the booth, whilst all the other belongings were waterlogged and gone. The car was brought to a workshop to be fixed and he quickly sold the Audi very cheaply. Rashid's father began to seek spiritual guidance in his difficult life.

Many years after that, when Rashid and his mother were talking about that car accident and how it had changed Rashid's father, Rashid told her that he thought the car had simply lost traction and hydroplaned on that wet road. However, she revealed to Rashid that seconds before the accident, both his parents had seen a tall shadowy figure crossing the road, an Orang Tinggi demon. It was at that moment, a repressed memory played in Rashid's mind and he shivered in fear, for he too, remembered seeing a large shadow passing by moments before the accident.

As for the car, Rashid still remembers the license plate. He has seen it a few times in workshops undergoing repairs for accidents. It had changed hands many times, and the last time Rashid saw it, someone had the car painted green.

The Kem

In the late 80s, Paddy and his friends became involved in the family side business, which was setting up tents for functions. These function tents were nothing like the marquee or the trendy tents available now these days. The tents were large and were set up by aligning heavy steel frame brackets at the top to form a rectangular shape and a bare roof structure which was then covered by heavy green tarpaulin. The sides of the tent structure were bare, which meant a cool breeze. Or if the guests were unfortunate, then rain would enter.

Metal chairs with hard plastic seats were arranged inside and a makeshift table was set up in the middle. The food would be arranged here for the guests. Later on, the metal chairs were replaced with plastic chairs. Rumours had it that a fatal brawl forced these changes.

The tents were used primarily to cater for guests at wedding functions. At other times, the tents were for funeral functions (doa arwah or tahlil) or thanksgiving prayer functions (doa selamat).

There was massive demand for these tents and it was lucrative business in Brunei. These were jobs that Paddy and his friends carried out after school.

They would haul all the components of the 'camp' or 'kem' (as they called it back then) into a long pickup truck. One of their friends was old enough to drive and he became the designated driver. Together, they formed a crew or a team. The family business had three teams, which allowed them to set up at a few locations in one night.

The job was very manual. It involved lifting the heavy metal bars together and assembling them to form the structure, whilst securing the meeting points or joints with rope. This was a precaution in case the weather turned out to be gusty.

The only safety equipment Paddy and his friends had were large oversized gloves, which they had to use to avoid getting metal (and rust) splinters.

It was fun to be with his friends at that time. They were together at work, setting up their 'kem' or tents, disassembling them the next evening. Of course, they went to school together and slept during classes together! It was their own brotherhood; they often joked around during work whilst smoking their cigarettes. Best of all, they got paid good money for what they saw as little manual work.

One evening, they had been asked to set up wedding tents for a family in a village near Jerudong. It was the typical evening set up; which was delayed usually by everyone's lax attitudes towards punctuality.

They ended up arriving at the wedding family's house much later than promised. Indifferent to the irate family, Paddy and his friends took out the metal frames and poles and started arranging them. Paddy and his friend, Abu, were carrying the long metal bar frame when suddenly, Abu kicked a rock and fell on the wet grass. Paddy laughed and joked if he thought the rock was a football.

Abu was not happy, he had intended to pick up the rock and throw it far away. His torchlight revealed it was not a rock but a small stone pillar.

"Is that a land surveyor's marking stone?" Abu asked.

Paddy looked hard and to his horror, it was not a landmark stone but a small worn-out gravestone! Paddy freaked out and dropped the metal frame on to the ground.

He looked around and could not believe how near it was to the house. Both Abu and him rushed to the house and explained to the family about the gravestone.

The head of the family, a middle-aged businessman, reassured them that it was nothing to worry about. It was the grave of one of their ancestors who was slain at a hill nearby. They were told that it was normal back then to bury relatives nearby so as to make visitations easier. The man suggested they just set up the tent away on the opposite side of the house compound. Paddy wished they had been told earlier about this. Now they had to move everything to the other side.

As Abu and himself walked back to the rest of the team, Paddy noticed one of the children in the house staring at them and pointing her finger at them. Paddy stared back at her in an attempt to scare her but the girl did not budge.

Throughout the night as the crew were setting up the wedding tents, they all joked about Abu and his gravestone kicking incident. They laughed raucously and Abu felt like a real old fool for not looking where he was walking.

After the tents had been set up, it was nearly well past midnight. They drove the long pickup truck back home.

The truck had seats for three, which included the driver. This meant that out of the crew of six, three had to stand up on the flatbed and hold on to the railings. This was hardly safe but nobody cared about HSE (Health Safety & Environment) back then. Smoking their cigarettes whilst one hand holding a railing tight as they rode into the wind was considered a manly thing for them. At least that was what these boys thought back then. As the truck drove through the narrow dark road at midnight, they jeered in excitement. This was brought to an abrupt end when the truck screeched to a halt.

Up ahead, they could see a white object lying flat in the middle of the road. Their driver friend told them to find out what it was and to move it. As they shone their torchlight beams on it, there was no doubt in everyone's mind of what it was. Wrapped in white cloth, it must be a corpse. Before they could ask each other what it was doing there, the white clothed corpse erected itself!

Although they could not see any face as everything was covered in white, they could feel the face of Death staring at them. The three guys standing behind and on the flatbed jumped out and scrambled into the front cab of the truck. No one was protesting how cramped the cabin was. They locked their doors shut and squeezed themselves to make their predicaments bearable.

"DRIVE!" Abu shouted at the driver. It was the logical thing to do. Their friend pushed the throttle to the metal and forced the diesel engine to bring them to their salvation.

They were tightly packed like sardines in a can and they drove as fast as they could, tolerating every bump in the road that was amplified and jolted through their bodies.

Paddy instinctively looked behind and he could see the white clothed corpse standing in the flatbed of that truck.

It was a ride to remember as they whimpered and cried in prayer to be delivered out of harm's way. There was no doubt this was a 'Tutut' ghost.

Eventually, the truck made its way to Manggis village and the Tutut disappeared. They all remained in the cab until Paddy's father came around and told them to stop their horseplay.

Paddy told his father what had happened. As a result, his friends were allowed to crash at his house that night. They could not sleep a wink and ended up sleeping after dawn. It meant that they had to skip school that day.

The next evening, the guys had to disassemble the tents and bring everything back home. They were not keen to visit that house again. This time they left earlier. When they arrived at the house, they could not disassemble the tents as the families had an impromptu after-party party. The crew were not happy, especially with one of the family members who was hogging the karaoke machine. It was very late by the time everything was settled. Paddy collected the payment and then they started the disassembling.

By this time, all the guests had left and the family members had gone in and called it a night. It was just Paddy and his crew in the large house compound. They were working unusually fast as they wanted to get out of there as soon as possible. Everyone felt an eerie feeling, as though they were being watched.

The crew began to hear the non-stop howling of dogs from around and everywhere.

"Come on, let's complete the job quickly!" Paddy tried to hurry his friends.

There was one last bar to pick up and secure into the truck. Everything else was already packed and ready to go.

Paddy and the others picked up the last long heavy metal bar frame and hauled it to the truck. As they got close to the truck, the bar had gotten much heavier on one side. Abu shouted at the others, "Stop playing games guys! This is not funny!"

Everyone was stricken with fear as they then watched the metal frame - which was as long as the flatbed of the truck - float in mid-air!

Abu was the first to shout out, "Tutut!" as he pointed to the white clothed corpse ghost which was standing behind their truck. The whole crew scrambled into the cab of the truck, squeezed into every possible space and drove off precariously back home. It was yet another unforgettable ride in the middle of the night.

Paddy's father and uncle were not happy that they had left the last metal frame at the house. However, the crew could not be persuaded to retrieve it even during broad daylight. Another team had to retrieve the last frame the next morning.

Paddy and his crew never went to that house again.

The Calling

Azrin was 22 years old when his father decided he should take up some responsibility with the family business, which was a small restaurant cafe in Beribi. His father had intentionally challenged him by lamenting out loudly that his youngest son, did not understand commitment and would find any excuse to get out of the new job. Azrin immediately knew he was being emotionally blackmailed. He now had to prove to his father that he could commit to a job no matter what the conditions were, especially if he wanted to have a better future role in management.

It was, by right, an easy job. His main role was to supervise the staff in the cafe. In addition to that, he would have to indulge in Public Relations (PR), which was essentially to pick up the occasional short banter with customers. He loved this part because it elevated his prestige. He would tell customers he was the owner of the cafe, without mentioning his father's sweat, blood and tears in setting up the establishment. More importantly, there was a task that only a trusted family member could do, which was to check and tally the daily earnings and then deposit that into the night deposit bank facility. This was done after he closed and secured the restaurant cafe every evening. The hours were long and he would have to wait for everyone to be done every night. By the time he got home, it was usually 12 midnight.

The initial rush and delight of the job quickly faded away. He yearned for the day his father would say there was an opening for him at the main office. He had only been in the job for two weeks and already he was regretting it. He could not complain to anyone, otherwise it would prove his father was right.

One evening, there was an incident involving a brawl at the restaurant cafe. There was no damage but the police had been called and witnesses were questioned. Azrin was not happy about this as it meant there was no business for a few hours and he could not close the restaurant and go home until the police had gone and everyone had settled down.

By the time everyone had gone, Azrin was very upset and started cursing about the job. He grumpily counted and then deposited the cafe earnings. He was keen to go home so he drove fast and a bit recklessly towards home.

Azrin was a smoker. He lit a cigarette whilst driving and blasted his R&B music out loud. He didn't care that it was 2am and he did not care about the residents who were supposedly sleeping soundly.

When Azrin got home, he got out of his car and lit another cigarette near the driveway. That was when he heard the sound. He was not sure what it was. The sound was difficult to interpret; it was like the cross between an owl's hooting and a woman's soft scream. Azrin felt spooked out.

He took a small flashlight and scanned the area of his house. In the back of his mind, Azrin thought it was a very bad idea to find out what it was. Perhaps he should let it be, whatever it was. As he turned around quickly, he saw a glint of light reflecting back. It was coming from his neighbour's house, where the bamboo plant had clumped together and grown very tall.

Without thinking, Azrin shone his light into the middle of the bamboo plant shrub. There, standing in the middle, he could see the figure of a ghastly looking woman with a white gown and long hair.

"Pontianak!" Azrin shouted out as he ran towards the front door of his house. He dropped the flashlight so hard that it broke on the ground.

He could hear an eerie scream as he jumped on the front porch. Azrin fumbled with his keys as he desperately started kicking the door, hoping someone would open the door in case he could not unlock the door in time.

He had a chain of keys - which included the restaurants, the cars and the house. He should have labelled the keys, he never thought his life would depend on it!

Time seemed to have slowed down as he rushed to figure out which key was his house key. He could not find the right key. Azrin felt his hands grow cold and then much colder. A grip on his left shoulder pulled him back. It was 'Game Over' for Azrin.

The vice grip immediately disappeared as Azrin fell down on the floor. The porch light had been switched on. His elder brother opened the door and asked what Azrin was doing on the floor. Azrin broke out in cold sweat, and his elder brother knew he should not ask at that time.

Azrin's father was never told what happened. Every evening, after business hours, Azrin would call home to make sure his elder brother or one of the other brothers would open the door when he arrived. He would never get out of the car until he saw his brother at the doorway.

Eventually, Azrin's brothers convinced the neighbour to cut down and remove the bamboo shrub as a precaution. Interestingly, they found that the bamboo plants seemed to be growing around an empty bare circle. This was not common for clumping bamboo plants. Some people say it was 'her home'.

The Fitting

Although I had no longer worked at the Intensive Care Unit (ICU), I would stay in contact with my former colleagues, whom I considered as my brethren. We often exchanged stories of our work experiences. They were keen to hear what I was doing in my life as a family physician. The stark differences between our current careers frequently caused us to ponder upon the career choices we made. One story they shared with me was about a patient who had an unusual medical situation.

Sham (not his real name), was a young 24-year-old engineer, who like most men in Brunei, loved to play football.

After work, he would meet up with his usual posse and they would play football at a local field. The football field had bright lights installed, which allowed them to play until 9pm.

One strange evening, in the midst of an exciting game, Sham confided to his friends that he did not feel his usual self. He said he felt unwell, and yet he felt as though there was someone else with him. To be precise, he used the phrase 'inside of him'. Soon after that, Sham felt he was engulfed by a darkness and lost consciousness, collapsing onto the soft ground.

His friends saw his entire body shake violently. They had never seen anything like that before. One of his friends muttered that it must be an epileptic fit. However, those who knew Sham very well knew he did not suffer from any ailments, let alone epilepsy. He was supposed to be as fit as a fiddle. And yet there he was having uncontrollable and continuous seizures.

Even when the paramedics arrived, the violent shaking of his body did not stop. When he was brought to the Accident & Emergency (A&E) Department of the hospital, the doctors there used all kinds of medication at their disposal to stop his fits. However, nothing worked. He had been fitting for more than an hour. Sham's parents and loved ones had formed a large crowd in the A&E department. Everyone was anxious and worried for Sham. He was a well-loved fellow and no one thought he deserved to be this unwell.

The doctors from the ICU were called. These interventionist doctors were the last line of hope. They promptly administered strong sedatives to induce an artificial coma. They passed a special tube down his throat so as to protect his airway whilst he was in a deep coma. This 'intubation tube' also allowed a respiratory life support machine to breathe for him.

In spite of the complete and deep sedation, Sham was still having continuous fits. They had used the maximal doses for the continuous infusion of medications to control his 'epileptic fit'. The doctors had started various investigations to find a cause for his illness, but everything including a CT brain scan, a spinal tap (lumbar puncture) and blood test results were all normal.

The doctors were puzzled on why he was still having seizures. To compound matters, they could not figure the cause of his seizures.

Sham had to be kept in constant 24-hours complete sedation and his body was dependent on the life support machine to breathe for him. This went on for a couple of days. Then the days turned into weeks! This got the doctors worried as they knew that prolonged uncontrolled seizures could lead to permanent brain damage. It was a frustrating time for everyone.

One day, whilst the doctors carried out their daily rounds to check on Sham, they saw Sham had lifted his left hand in the air, as though he was saluting. He was still unconscious! The doctors laughed it off, but truthfully, they were freaked out by it. The drugs that Sham was continuously receiving via intravenous infusion were not only powerful sedatives but also potent muscle relaxants, which should have induced complete paralysis of his body. And yet Sham's arm had moved on its own as though mocking the doctors.

One of Sham's relatives who happened to be a doctor, decided to contact a traditional healer. The traditional healer; a wise lady from West Malaysia, flew to Brunei and started her treatment on the poor unconscious Sham. After 4 days, Sham's seizures had stopped. Within a week, he no longer needed to be in an induced coma or to be on life support. He was soon discharged and went home without any incident or permanent disability.

The healer lady told the doctors that Sham had unwittingly kicked a 'child Jinn' or child spirit whilst playing football during Maghrib prayer time. The father of the child Jinn was furious and had gone after Sham. She said it was a difficult task to convince 'the father' to leave Sham's body. Luckily, 'it' was eventually persuaded to leave Sham in peace.

From time to time, the ICU doctors would talk about the strange case and found it hard to believe why it had happened.

As for Sham, when he was settled at home, the healer visited him. She counseled him and advised him to be very careful when playing football at night. Since that incident, Sham does not dare to play football at night any more.

The On-call Room

A few doctors who have had to work overnight at the hospital in Kuala Belait (KB) town, shared with me their encounters with a particular 'on-call' room.

The hospital doctors who are posted in KB town are usually expatriate doctors. They have to stay at the allocated hospital (on-call) rooms until more permanent housing has been provided.

On other occasions, physicians from the other districts have to work there to replace the usual doctor who is either on vacation, sick leave or is awaiting for their new working contract. Since on-call work or work after hours extend through the night and until the next day, the doctors are provided with an on-call room for them to rest and sleep.

One story I was told came from a physician who has since left the country.

Ramy was an Indian expat physician who had just arrived in Brunei. It was his first time being in Southeast Asia. He had been told that he would be posted at the KB hospital. He didn't know much about Brunei and had no idea where Kuala Belait town was. He thought it would not make much of a difference where he was working as Brunei is such a small country (compared to India) so it must be the same conditions everywhere.

Since his government housing had not been arranged, he was given residence at the hospital on-call room until the proper housing arrangement had been finalised. He was told it would take several weeks.

He thought the on-call room looked reasonable. It was not too shabby. After all, he had worked in places that were far worse. The on-call room was situated at the edge of the hospital grounds, which was good as it gave him privacy.

Ramy made sure he kept himself busy as he didn't want to be on his own. He was worried he would end up feeling homesick as he was already missing his family. Although his work burden was much less than in other busy hospitals, he found the hours were quite long and lonely.

Occasionally, when he entered his on-call room, he would notice subtle oddities, as though something was displaced but he could not figure out what it was. Perhaps he was too busy to be bothered by it then. Sometimes, when he entered the room after a long shift, he would notice how cold it was. Other times, he heard voices of people talking. He dismissed that and thought perhaps some of the night staff were secretly smoking outside and were having their usual banter.

One evening, Ramy was walking into the hallway leading to his on-call room when he noticed a woman walking in front of him. Her slender back was facing him. He assumed that she was a nurse as she was dressed in white. He did not bother to look at her so he kept his eyes glued to the floor as he did not want to strike up conversation. He was dead tired. As he opened the door, he noticed in the corner of his eye that the nurse seemed to have gone through the wall!

He turned to see and saw there was no one there. Ramy thought it must have been an optical illusion. She must have gone into the other room. It was really none of his business, he thought. Ramy did not think much of it. That night, he had a nightmare. He dreamt he was trapped in the hallway and could not get out, as none of the doors or room would open. When he woke up, Ramy's clothes were drenched in sweat and he was late for work!

The next evening, when Ramy was heading back to his room, he saw a woman walking in front of him. He assumed it was the same person. As he got in front of his door, he paused and looked to his left, and watched the woman walked straight into a wall and disappeared!

Ramy was horrified. He ran into his room and closed the door. He calmed himself down and reasoned that even if what he saw was true, by right, the situation should not be of any consequence to him or his life. Eventually, he reasoned it was probably a trick of the tired sad mind. He thought about his homesickness and figured he must be having visual hallucinations secondary to his suboptimal mood. He wondered if he was having clinical depression.

He did his best to get to his on-call room early and sleep in early. After that evening, he had not seen anything else.

However, things changed when one late night, he was kept very busy as there was a terrible multiple car road traffic accident.

By the time he got to his room, it was already 2am in the morning. Ramy crashed into his bed. He needed to sleep as he had to start early the next day. Although he was quite tired, the adrenaline had kept him awake. He tried to close his eyes for a few minutes, but he could not fall asleep. His nose felt itchy; he rubbed his nose and felt there was something on it. He opened his eyes and to his horror, he saw a pale woman in a white gown snarling at him from the ceiling. Her long black hair had extended down to his face and near his nose.

Ramy wanted to jump out of the bed and run, but he was paralysed by fear as his body trembled and his heart palpitated uncontrollably. He recited a mantra repeatedly until slowly the woman on the ceiling had disappeared.

After that incident, Ramy moved out of the on-call room and stayed at one of his colleague's house. He persuaded the hospital administrators to expedite his housing arrangement or he would resign. He never returned to the on-call room. Within three weeks, Ramy moved in to a new house.

Interestingly, a few other doctors who had the displeasure of staying at the room mentioned they occasionally saw a white streak cross that same hallway. Others had told me that they noticed chairs and other objects had been moved whilst they were fast asleep. However, none had the up close and personal encounter as Ramy's, which was fortunate for them.

Teluki

One of my readers had suggested that I write about the 'Teluki'. She, herself, hailed from Ukong Village in Tutong, and although it was her suggestion, she was reluctant to talk about it. I thought this was a very strange behaviour. I wonder if it was because she was afraid of 'cabul' i.e. conjuring the spirit through talking about it. Anyway, she suggested I look up on YouTube for a video about it. Some guy had made a short low budget movie about it.

That some guy turned out to be my friend, Abdul Zainidi. Abdul Zainidi is a film-maker, who usually makes 'shorts' or short movies and he has appeared in the Cannes film festival and is frequently invited and involved in film festivals all over the world.

He made a short low budget movie called 'Teluki'. Armed with a handheld digital camera, he interviewed those who were involved and then filmed a separate movie.

The original story is different from the movie, as it was adapted as per request from the families as well as to suit the (zero) budget of the film. I would recommend watching it.

The Youtube url can be found at the end.

Abdul Zainidi told me that his grandparents were the ones who first told him about the incident involving the 'Teluki' spirit.

His grandfather has had the 'sight' ever since he chopped down a large tree deep in Ukong jungle. At that time, he did not know the tree was the home of a temperamental 'Bunian' or jungle spirit. He had also suffered from a (cardiovascular) stroke, which affected him on a daily basis. He was able to see the 'Bunian' jungle spirits from time to time whenever he entered the jungle.

Abdul Zainidi's grandmother was born 'gifted'. She was able to see the spirits within the vicinity and from a different locality.

This is their story.

***

It was 1992. Ukong village is a village deep in rural Tutong district of Brunei. The village was known for its sago production, which was slowly growing against the dense and thick jungles of Ukong.

One evening, villagers had noticed that the night was not as dark as usual. In fact, it had a pink hue in the night sky. There was little light pollution in the rural area which made it even stranger. Locals would say it was not a good omen.

The next day, three children from two families were playing near the edge of the jungle, which was behind their house.

They were aged 6, 8 and 12 years old and were enjoying their free time as it was their school holidays.

They heard a whistling sound, which sounded like a 'seruling' or a flute, being played in the jungle. One of the neighbours had seen the children enter the jungle, which was not an abnormal thing to do as children.

It was at this time, Abdul Zainidi's grandmother saw a vision of the dark essence of the jungle - the Teluki spirit calling out to the children. She ran out to find them but she was too far away and it was too late.

The children had been swallowed up by the jungle.

Over the next few days, villagers had organised themselves into search parties to look for the missing children. Abdul Zainidi's grandfather was part of the search party.

As they scoured through the Ukong jungle, his grandfather saw glimpses of the Teluki. It would appear in different forms. Sometimes he would encounter it as a strange-looking child with white eyes, whilst at other times, he saw what was best described as a black mist with a large eye object in the middle of it.

Several shamans had volunteered themselves with the search parties. A few of them were brave enough to tell the parties that their spiritual searches indicated the children were already dead. They would mention the Teluki spirit had captured them and consumed their souls. It was hard for them as they were often then confronted by angry relatives.

Eventually, one of the children was found. At least the body was found in a river.

There are two account versions of what was found.

Some have said that the headless body was found in a river. The 'severed' head of the 12-year-old child was found on a riverbank. The body had been completely drained of blood and the head did not look like it was cut, but more like pulled away from the body. None of the villagers were forensic experts but they all agreed that it did not look like a cut of a human (with or without a cutting machine).

Others disputed this and said that the pale child's body was found in a river, with his head intact. Those who believed this version thought the child was lured to drown himself in the river.

Weeks later, they called off the search as they could not find any trace of the other two children.

Relatives had asked Abdul Zainidi's grandmother for spiritual insight, particularly about the demon that had taken the children. She mentioned that the Teluki spirit was one that had lived in the jungle for a very long time. She had known about it ever since she was a child. Generations before her knew about the Teluki, which was the dark vengeful essence of the jungle spirit, seeking to destroy Man for encroaching its jungle, by killing children. It would ensnare children into the jungle. At times, it would leave strange trinkets nearby the jungle to lure them.

The disappearance of the children devastated both families. In the end, both families moved away from Ukong. Their other relatives, however, had stayed on - reminding their own children to be aware of the Ukong jungle and more importantly, the Teluki spirit.

***

When I first heard about this story, I was quite shocked on discovering how 'recent' this happening had occurred. People who end up missing in the jungle now these days lead to a national inter-agency search. I wonder if this story was actually hiding the works of a psychopathic killer?

I had an interesting discussion with Abdul Zainidi about this and it was also one of his theories about the happenings. Of course, he can't deny his grandparents' accounts. He also mentioned that very strange things had occurred during the filming of his Teluki video.

You can check the link here: https://youtu.be/ClLyoAOlY5c

Abdul Zainidi has made a film series titled Vanishing Children. This film series has been screened at several international film festivals. He aims to write and film a new story based on the Teluki spirit incident with better budget and fresh insights.

About The Author

Aammton Alias is a practising medical doctor. For the past 17 years, he has worked in a variety of hospitals, hospices and intensive care units. He continued to be a passionate family physician in a small town. Now, he is embarking on a whole new adventure.

He is an advocate for those who seek his help, and his compassion has made him an activist of various causes. He is also a writer, a poet warrior, an entrepreneur at heart and most importantly, he is a family man.

You can reach him via:
Twitter: @Aammton
Telegram: @ElTonyX
Instagram: @aammton
Facebook Page: www.fb.me/aammtonalias

My Other Books

Please do check out some of my other books:

Real Ghost Stories of Borneo

Real Ghost Stories of Borneo is a collection of over 30 short ghost stories, written by a family physician working in Borneo. These supernatural tales are genuine accounts with a unique insight into the local population and what ails them. Be warned, very few of these stories have a 'happily ever after' ending. A number of these stories may appear to have been left open ended with no explanation. The stories were shared with the author in that manner.

Please note slightly different title on Amazon.com
www.amazon.com/dp/1717062326

The Last Bastion of Ingei: Imminent

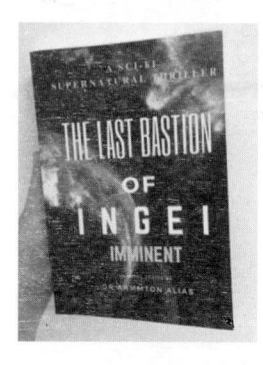

On the mysterious island of Borneo, three conservationists work together, battling against the odds. Their mission, to stop poachers from exploiting the endangered wildlife from being hunted and sold, key amongst them, the prized, enigmatic and rare 'Pangolin'. However, they are themselves being stalked by a far greater menace than they could ever imagine. The jungle hides its secret well, but the friends are about to confront an ancient menace, far older than humanity itself, an old foe long since forgotten. Soon, the fate of Mankind will hang in the balance. Meanwhile, a captain in the elite 5th Recon Unit is brought back to face an unspoken tragedy that no one believes happened, whilst elsewhere, recent supernatural events re-activate a secretive vanguard for human salvation: The LIMA

www.ingei.b1percent.com

The Last Bastion of Ingei: DAY 1 to DAY 4

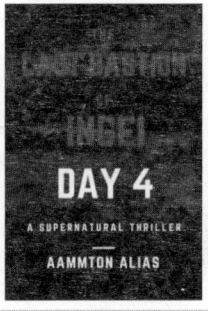

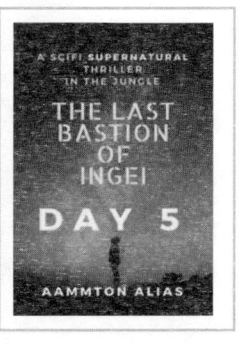

Available at:
http://www.day1.b1percent.com
http://www.day2.b1percent.com
http://www.day3.b1percent.com
http://www.day4.b1percent.com
http://www.day5.b1percent.com

Be The One Percent: Unlock Secrets to True Success, Real Wealth & Ultimate Happiness

http://www.book.b1percent.com

The King And The Minister

http://www.king.b1percent.com

The Vessel of Our Writing Dreams: Where Do Our Ideas Come From

http://www.vessel.b1percent.com

LET ME GO! How to Get Off Unwanted WhatsApp Chat Groups For Good

www.wtfrak.b1percent.com

Now Everyone Can Write And Publish A Book In 3 Days

http://www.write.b1percent.com

How I Became a Self-Published Author: The Journey to 51,000 Word

Published by MPH
www.mph1.b1percent.com

http://www.mphonline.com/books/nsearchdetails.aspx?&pcode=9789674153786

Stop Press!

Just a few things to say right at the end of the book. We are expecting to produce the 3rd Real Ghost Stories of Borneo book some time in the later half of 2019. We would like to follow a theme for this book, though the stories that turn up do come from different events and scenes.

Ideally for the third book, we would like to explore uniformed services experiences, in particular (but not limited to) SAF or Singapore Armed Forces in the jungles of Brunei. At the same time, we would like to hear more stories to related to maritime supernatural encounters.

We intend to hold a contest for the best original ghost stories submitted and published. We have not yet decide on the prizes, but we will try our best to make it worthwhile.

The rules for the contest and stories submission are that you should write a true ghost story based on your personal experience or the experience of someone you personally know. Geolocation is important, meaning that the stories must be from locations within Borneo (Brunei, Sabah, Sarawak and Kalimantan).

There is no fixed word limit, but we do expect a minimum of 500 words. We may edit your story to make it suitable for the book. You can also submit any appropriate photos and/ or illustrations.

Of course, submitting a story may not mean that we will publish your story for this book. We may, however, publish for the next book after that. In any case, we will inform you before we do that.

If you do not wish to write a story, you can contact us by contacting the author through email and social media (Instagram, Facebook & Telegram etc) and we can convert our conversation into a meaningful story. You can choose to submit your stories anonymously or we can credit your name to the story.

The copyright of the book and the submitted published stories will belong to M Content Creations company and Dr. Aammton Alias.

We reserve the right to edit and rewrite the submitted stories as deemed necessary.

Please do contact:

Telegram: @ElTonyX

Instagram: @aammton

Facebook Page: www.fb.me/aammtonalias

This is a teaser for an upcoming graphic book version of the Real Ghost Stories of Borneo 1.

Keep on the lookout for further developments in 2019.